THREE O'CLOCK
SHERRI WARD

THREE O'CLOCK
SHERRI WARD

ISBN-13: 978-0-692-37396-5
ISBN-10: 0-692-37396-9
Library of Congress Control Number: 2015904511

Butterfly Feet Publishing
Fort Collins, Colorado, USA
butterflyfeetpublications.com

Therefore, my beloved brethren, be steadfast, immovable, always abounding in the work of the Lord, knowing that your toil is not in vain in the Lord.

1 Corinthians 15:58, NASB

Chapter 1

Bob listened to the sound of birds chirping outside his office window. One melodic song in particular drew his attention. *Is that a meadowlark?* He stared out the window for a few minutes but didn't see the bird he was looking for. With a weary sigh, he turned back to his computer. "Don't want to do this any more. I just don't," he muttered as he clacked away at the keyboard.

After a moment he pushed his keyboard back. Standing up, he stretched and stared out the window for a while. Then he turned his gaze toward the large clock on the wall. It was nearing only two in the afternoon. *Plenty of time to get some work done later.* Taking the few short steps to his office door, he glanced furtively out into the hallway. Satisfied that the few coworkers in the hall were intent on their own business, he closed the door quietly and returned to his desk. The project he had been halfheartedly working on was still open on his computer, but after a moment's hesitation, he saved and closed it. *I should probably check email.*

Instead, he opened an internet game.

Nearly an hour later there was a light knock on the door, so Bob quickly closed the game window and opened his email program. Then he got up and opened the door. He was not too surprised to see The Manager standing there.

With a friendly smile The Manager asked, "Bob, how's it going? How's that project we talked about this morning coming along?"

"Fine, everything's just fine!" Bob smiled and nodded, but his thoughts contradicted his words. *Nothing's going right, nobody replies to my emails and this is never going to get done on time. What's more, I don't care because nobody appreciates my efforts anyway, and I'm tired. I don't want to do this anymore. I'd rather play internet games. And besides all that, Charlie, that mentor you assigned to coach me, is a pompous jerk who treats me like I'm stupid!* Bob remained mute, blinking innocently and trying to appear serene and confident as he waited for The Manager's reply.

The Manager watched Bob perceptively for several moments before he answered, "That project's very important, critical actually, and we need to have it done on time!" He paused before adding, "You know, you have several incomplete projects that you still need to finish up."

"Yes, I know." Bob nodded again but couldn't help shifting his eyes away from The Manager's steady gaze.

"Let's not be short-sighted. The day is getting on. The Door won't stay open forever!"

As The Manager walked away, Bob returned to his desk, this time leaving his office door ajar. He started to peck away at the keyboard again, checking for new emails. "The Door, always the Door!" he grumbled quietly. "And what does he mean by 'short-sighted' anyway? And projects – always overdue or not good enough! Doesn't he ever notice the real and actual work I do around this lousy place?"

Immediately he felt a sharp twinge of guilt as he remembered something The Manager had said to him that very morning. *Bob, I want you to know I appreciate your work. I understand that things aren't always easy around here, but the report you finished up and turned in this morning was detailed, accurate and right on time. Good job!*

Footsteps in the hall alerted Bob that The Manager had returned. Relieved he had not reopened the internet game, he looked up from the monitor. "Yes, Sir?"

"Bob, you look tired. Is there anything you need help with?"

Bob tried to look thoughtful as he replied with a slight shake of his head, "No, I really don't think so. Everything's fine, just fine." As he gave The Manager a deliberately blank stare, he had a moment's thought that he really ought to come clean and tell him that things actually were not fine at all and that he probably could use some help. His pride welled up at the thought. *If I ask for help, he will think I'm inept and not up to the challenge. It's not like I'm stupid or something. I can do this! But somehow I just don't feel like it. Besides, if I told him anything I would probably end up telling him Charlie's a jerk.*

The Manager continued to study Bob intently for a long moment before he finally said, "You know the break room has refreshment, perhaps a break would do you good." With that, he walked away again.

Bob leaned back in his chair with a sigh. He'd been to the break room several times already. He didn't want more caffeine and donuts. He also didn't want to keep working. He looked again out the window. It was a beautiful sunny afternoon with hardly a cloud in the sky. Wildflowers dotted the grassy hillside just beyond the parking lot. A gentle breeze ruffled the leaves of the few trees on the hill. Birds were singing. "A short nap on the grass, that's what I really need," he muttered to himself.

Ignoring the call of the meadowlarks, he turned once again back to his work. A few more keyboard clicks revealed that a particular email he needed still wasn't in his inbox. "Drat! Idiots!" he exclaimed angrily. "This is not my fault! How can I be expected to get anything done? Stupid internet! Stupid people and their stupid, pig-headed agendas!" Suddenly remembering that the door was still open, he tightened his lips and hoped no one had heard his angry outburst.

A new email suddenly arrived in his inbox. A quick look at the title revealed that it still was not what he needed. In fact, it was from Charlie, and Bob scowled as he read the title of the message. 'AS SOON AS YOU GET THIS' all in caps. Charlie's messages usually contained titles and text asserting urgency, but Bob had learned they rarely were anything all that important. It seemed that attaching urgency to his messages was merely one of Charlie's ways to prove his superiority. *'AS SOON AS YOU GET THIS?' Well, maybe that's the problem, Charlie, maybe I simply didn't receive that particular message at all!* Instead of opening the message, he clicked the box to select it, and then hit the delete button. He figured he would retrieve it from the trash folder and read it later, but for now it felt good to emphatically and defiantly ignore it.

Once again he started to mutter quietly to himself. "This has been enough work! It's been a long day already! I wish I could go home!" But the clock on the wall seemed to mock him as it showed him the time, now only three in the afternoon. *Three o'clock? Why can't it be five o'clock? If it were five o'clock, I could get out of here! I'm tired, tired, tired, don't want to do this anymore!*

3

As he continued to stare at the clock, his thoughts began to drift. He recalled that when he had first begun with The Company, the time flew by quickly and 5:00 p.m. sometimes went unnoticed because he was so intent on the work in front of him. That seemed so long ago. He had been so happy to be working for The Company back then. *What a contrast to how I feel today!*

Trying to dismiss his uneasy thoughts, he turned and again looked out the window at the grassy hillside. *Surely no one would miss me if I just slipped outside for a little while to lie down on the soft grass.* Standing up, he yawned and stretched, then headed for the break room.

Once there, he walked toward the vending machine in the back of the room. Leaning against it with one arm over his head, he peered through the glass and studied the little bottles inside. *If this machine had ordinary stuff like chips and colas it might get more attention. People might actually select something from it once in a while. Those little bottles are just weird.*

As he turned away from the vending machine, he felt a sudden cold chill. He thought he caught a glimpse of a black-cloaked figure leaving the room. He also thought he heard a faint laugh. Well, no matter. He had work to finish at his desk. He grabbed another cup of coffee and a stale donut, but before he could make his exit, a coworker entered the room. Bob had the strange sensation of the cold chill returning with him. Shrugging it off, he greeted him with, "Hey, Mark, what's happening?"

"Well, nothing new, that's for sure." Mark sighed. "Same old, same old…" He made his way slowly to the vending machine, hands in pockets. After a spurious glance at the contents, he turned away to the coffee and donuts. "Hey, Bob, you get in any good pranks lately?" Mark's bored expression turned to one of amusement as he fixed himself a cup of coffee.

"Nah! That last prank we pulled – I think it nearly cost us our jobs!"

"Yeah!" Mark laughed and nodded as they both thought back.

That day Bob had just happened to be passing Mark's office when Mark cheerfully called out to him, "Yo, Bob! Come in here a minute. Take a look at this email I got!"

After reading the message displayed on Mark's monitor, Bob let his breath out slowly and said, "Whew! Hey, you aren't going to click on that link, are you?"

"Nah, you think I'm nuts?" Mark scoffed. "But I think I'll send it to someone – you know, as a joke. Come on, who could we send it to?"

Bob laughed, but then said soberly, "Hold on, Mark, that might not be such a good idea. What if they actually click on the link?"

"Well, what if they do, and it turns out to be legit, and they get rich, and they want to thank us for sending the email, and they give us lots and lots of money and…"

Bob laughed. "Whoa, dude, like that's going to happen!"

"Yeah, I know, but still, it could be funny just to send it on. How 'bout Amy? Let's send it to her! She opens all her junk mail, and even clicks on the links!"

"Nah, I don't think that's such a good idea. Let's just change the wallpaper on her desktop, you know, like we did to Gerald once; that was a good one!" Bob laughed, then soberly added, "And it was harmless enough, you know, nobody got hurt."

"Yeah, that was hilarious!" Mark admitted with a chuckle. "We removed all his desktop icons and replaced the wallpaper with a screenshot of the previous wallpaper and the icons. I thought he was going to wear himself out trying to click on the new wallpaper icons and they weren't really icons, just that stupid picture!" They both laughed, but then Mark persisted, "But we did that already! We need to do something new, and besides, I just hate to see an opportunity for a good prank go to waste!"

In the end, Mark didn't listen to Bob's words of caution, and the email with its promise of a grand fortune was forwarded first to Mark's anonymous personal email account, and then directly to Amy. Then they hurried to her office and waited quietly just outside the door, hoping to find out just how effective their little practical joke had been. At first they heard nothing out of the ordinary, but before long a small wail of distress followed by mild cursing assured them she likely had not only opened the email but even clicked on the link. They casually walked into her office as though they just happened to be walking by.

"Something wrong, Amy?" Mark asked innocently.

"Yes! I mean, no! And if there is, I don't know what it is!" She looked at them defensively, and in her state of panic she failed to notice the deliberately innocent stares they were giving her. "I think – well, you see, there was this email – and I clicked on a link – and now look, I can't get my computer to do anything at all! I am no longer in control of the mouse, and I can't even shut down this website I got redirected to, and now I don't know what to do." Amy stared helplessly at her monitor.

Although the men exchanged knowing smiles, Bob was feeling an underlying remorse for the havoc they had caused. His smile faded as he approached Amy and her computer. "Have you tried 'control-alt-delete'?"

"Of course I have! I can't even shut the darn thing off with the button – see this?" She demonstrated by punching the on/off button on her computer repeatedly. "Nothing!"

Mark could no longer control himself and burst out laughing.

"Don't laugh, this isn't funny! Why is Mark laughing?" Amy's suspicions were finally beginning to kick in.

Mark composed himself, saying innocently, "I guess I'm just in a good mood today, what can I say?" Then he crouched on the floor and unplugged the computer. After a few moments he plugged it back in and they all stared at the monitor only to find a blank blue screen staring back at them. Now even Mark looked sober.

Amy glared at the two of them. "Did you guys have something to do with this? Why did you just now happen to come to my office? What did you guys do? Did you send me that email?"

Mark shook his head as a warning to Bob not to say anything, but Bob was done with the joke. He was already thinking ahead as to what the consequences might be. However, a sense of defensive justification was also rising up inside. "Alright," he said, "but all we did was forward you an email. You're the one dumb enough to not only open it but even click on the link!" He regretted the words as soon as they were out of his mouth, but he stuck his chin out defiantly in spite of his remorse.

Amy stared at him for a moment in stunned silence, and then with a seething calm she asked, "I'm dumb? Do you have anything else awful you'd like to say about me?"

"Yeah, Bob, what other awful things do you want to say about Amy?" Mark chimed in.

Bob glared at Mark resentfully. "Shut up! This whole thing was your idea!"

The tension was unmistakable, and for a moment no one spoke. Then Mark said, "Look Amy, we didn't think you'd actually click on the link. It was just supposed to be a joke."

"Yeah, well jokes are supposed to be funny. This is not funny. My computer is broken and I'll probably get fired, and it's totally your fault!"

"I gotta get back to work. Call IT. They'll fix it for you." With that Mark walked out, and after mumbling a quick apology, Bob left as well.

The end of the day found all three in The Manager's office. The Company's firewall had been breached with nearly disastrous consequences, and naturally The Manager was not pleased. He added a new requirement to their work load, and that was to take an internet safety course offered by The Company.

Since that time, Amy's resentment toward the guilty pair had subsided and she had begun once again to speak civilly to them. Bob was glad because he liked Amy and didn't want to lose her friendship. However, he had a sense that some of the trust The Manager had placed in him was eroded, and he wasn't sure it could ever be restored. He retained a lingering sense of guilty sadness.

Now, as Bob and Mark stood in the break room, the memory left them both speechless for a few moments. Bob decided to change the subject. "Work going okay?" Although he asked, he didn't really care, thinking only that he should get back to his own work. He edged slowly toward the door.

Mark, however, was eager to talk. "No, not really. I mean, it's either that my computer is screwed up, or the people I email don't think my concerns are important enough to get back to me. You know, we're supposed to all pull together here, right? But it's like my problems and projects don't mean a thing to anyone else!"

Bob sighed heavily. "Yeah, pretty much the same here. Then when you finally do get a response, it's never exactly what you need. Everybody wants to procrastinate and nobody can make a decision to save their life! Either that or they make all the decisions and then take all the credit if something worthwhile actually results!" He thought of adding a few choice words about Charlie, but he prided himself on not being a gossip, and he also realized as he was standing there that he didn't really trust

Mark enough to share any specific details with him anyway.

"Yeah, meantime, we're busting our butts! There's times I'm not sure this is worth all the effort, ya know?"

"Yeah, nothin's ever easy around here, that's for sure!"

Mark lowered his voice and confided cautiously, "Well, I for one am thinking of not staying on, know what I mean?" Bob nodded but didn't reply, so Mark continued, "I just would rather get on with things as they were before I started here. I can't say I ever really felt fulfilled, or that whatever work I did ever seemed to matter all that much, but on the other hand, I didn't have all this stress and obligation and difficulty, either. And besides that, somehow now I just feel tired and bored with it all."

"I can't say I completely disagree with you," Bob nodded. "I'm feeling pretty tired of it all myself."

The negative conversation was leaving Bob feeling gloomier than ever. He took a bite from the donut he was still holding and tossed the rest of it into the trash. After a quick gulp of the coffee, he poured the rest into the sink and tossed the cup. Then, with a weary sigh, he said indifferently to Mark, "Well, don't work too hard." Then he headed out into the hall, intending to get back to his office.

He had only been walking for a moment when he changed his mind. *Maybe having a look at the projects in my drawer will somehow help matters. Maybe just the walk to the Great Hallway will help me feel energized, even motivated!* He turned and headed in that direction instead.

When he got to the Great Hallway, he stopped briefly to gaze down the length of it. At the very end of it was The Door. It was actually a double door, larger and more magnificent than any he had ever seen. Covered in glittery gold, it covered the entire end wall. It was always partly open, but the only thing visible through the slight opening was an intensely bright white light. Bob had never seen anyone even approach The Door too closely, let alone actually go through it. He had heard that The Manager did go freely through The Door, and some even claimed to have seen angelic beings go through. Not having seen that for himself, he sometimes doubted it, especially lately. Still, as he did even now, he always had a sense of awe whenever he stopped to gaze at it.

He turned his attention back to the hall itself. Both walls of the long hall were lined by an elaborate set of ornate drawer fronts, the cabinets of which were built right in to the wall itself. The drawer fronts were made of shiny brass with decorative embossing. Each employee of The Company had his own drawer, and the employee names were inscribed on name plates on each drawer front. A mere touch on a small fingerprint recognition pad unlocked the drawer, allowing access to the projects and files within.

When an employee had a finished project he either delivered it to The Manager in person, or he brought it here and placed it into his drawer. Often the project remained until more projects were added, but other times as soon as the drawer was closed again, there was a whooshing sound indicating that whatever projects were in the drawer were being conveyed away through the hidden channel behind the drawers.

After unlocking his drawer, Bob leafed briefly through the papers inside. Then he closed the drawer, which automatically locked again. With a sigh he glanced once more toward the Door before turning away and heading back toward his office. *Maybe I can just print out that unfinished project I'm supposed to be working on and bring it and put it in the drawer and see what happens. It may not be exactly finished but I have done some hard work on it.*

He remembered a day quite some time ago when a coworker had apparently been having similar thoughts. It had been quite a spectacle. The man had approached his drawer slowly, carrying what appeared to be a completed assignment. The really strange part about the incident was that there had been two very mysterious individuals with him who were cloaked with long, hooded black garments from head to floor and who walked with heads down, faces not visible. They loomed over the little man, one on either side keeping him sandwiched between them, almost leaning on him as they walked. They seemed to be quite firmly pressing him toward his drawer with his stack of papers. At one point he seemed to change his mind because he tried to turn around, but they held him fast as they talked fervently, one into each ear, yet too quietly for Bob to hear. The trio finally stopped in front of the man's drawer. After another moment of hesitation, the man unlocked and opened the drawer and then placed the stack inside. Then he quickly closed the drawer, and finally the cloaked figures let up on him, allowing him to turn and start to walk away.

Suddenly The Manager had appeared, and with a short, vehement, "Be gone!" he had dismissed the two in black. Without any protest they had glided away silently. The Manager had then looked sadly at the worker, and asked gently, "George, is this the best you can do? Are you sure that project is finished?"

"Uh, yes, I believe it is – uh, finished," George had stammered, staring down at his own feet.

"Well, let's see, shall we? Open the drawer." George had reluctantly complied, and The Manager produced a shiny gold lighter from his pocket. As he held it over the contents of George's drawer, the lighter sparked, and George had cried out and jumped back as the project he had just placed into the drawer quickly turned to tinder feeding a flaming spire. In moments there was nothing left but a smoldering trace of black ash. George had collapsed on the floor, sobbing pathetically.

Meredith, the front office receptionist, had watched the frightening incident as well, standing at Bob's elbow. "Blank paper," she had whispered. "He tried to cover up blank paper with a title page and a few meaningless diagrams." Bob hadn't questioned how Meredith knew that. She always seemed to know things that were not necessarily apparent to others.

Now as he walked back toward his office, Bob remembered some things that hadn't seemed significant to him at the time. Like the color of George's uniform. It wasn't spotlessly white, it was gray. He had come to notice soon after he'd been hired that there were quite a few workers with gray uniforms, and there were some noticeable differences in their behavior. The most obvious difference was that they seemed to avoid The Manager whenever possible, often simply turning and walking in the other direction if they happened to see him. And although they generally kept up the appearance of being busy, especially when in the presence of The Manager, it didn't seem that they ever accomplished much that was really useful.

At first, Bob couldn't understand their attitudes. Rather than being thankful for a job in The Company, they complained a lot about work in general. They were also quick to criticize the efforts of other employees, and to blame others when things went awry. Bob had been so excited to be working for The Company that at first he had just ignored the

10

malcontents. Lately, however, they were the very ones he found himself talking to and even agreeing with. The realization made him feel troubled.

Now as he thought about these things, his thoughts returned to how very thankful and happy he himself had been as a brand new employee.

Prior to being hired, he had always secretly admired The Company, although he had never really thought he could become a part of it. He walked by it every day on his way to his own menial job at the downtown diner, usually with Sam, his fellow disgruntled co-worker. As they walked, they had a habit of ribbing each other about different things. When they walked by The Company, the kidding would turn to each challenging the other to walk in and apply for a job.

The front office of The Company was lined with large windows, and like kids in front of a candy store, they always slowed down a little to look inside. The spacious front office and reception area was beyond orderly, it seemed to beckon with the comforts of an elegant home. The office receptionist, an older woman with white hair and reading glasses, was usually seated behind the reception desk. She always seemed occupied with the computer or phones or people, and she was always crisply presentable in a spotless white uniform.

The morning before Bob actually did walk in and apply had started out just like all those other days. As usual, the receptionist didn't even look up as they stood staring through the window. And as usual, Sam was poking Bob as he said with a jovial smirk, "Come on, Bob! You should just walk right in there and submit your application! They need you with all your fine dishwashing experience!" He laughed as if it had been the first time he had joked like that.

Bob had retorted, "You're the one they need – someone to show them how to flip burgers on the grill!" And then, just like every other day, they had turned away from the window and headed up the street toward the diner.

Just like every other day – but suddenly, it wasn't. This time, before they had reached the end of the block, a voice called out from behind them. "Turn around!"

Startled, they did turn around, and were perplexed to see the receptionist standing just outside The Company, holding the door open as she looked directly at them.

They stared at her speechlessly for a moment, and then Bob called back, "What?"

"Turn around!" was all she said again, and with that she walked back into the building, closing the door behind her.

Bewildered, they continued to stare at the closed door for a moment, and then Sam laughed heartily. "Yeah, Bob, turn around, walk right in there and submit your application!" He laughed again, but this time the laughter sounded hollow, and then abruptly he said irritably, "Come on, we're late already." He turned and headed up the street, not even looking to see if Bob followed.

Bob continued to stare at the closed door. "Late for what?" he muttered to himself. "Another day of washing dishes, and, if I'm lucky, bussing tables!" He sighed bleakly.

Almost inexplicably, his thinking progressed. *Was it really so unattainable to become an employee of the best company in town? Was it absolutely impossible? What if I do, in fact, walk in there and apply for a job? At least then I'd know just how stringent the requirements really are. What do I have to lose anyway? A little pride. Big deal. I'll certainly be no worse off than I am now. On the other hand, what do I stand to gain if the impossible happens and they offer me a job?* The possibilities were beyond imagination. As he stood there, he suddenly realized he'd made a decision. Tomorrow he would not dress for washing dishes. He would dress in his best, and he would walk through that door. Bob watched the closed door for another moment before he turned and hurried to catch up with Sam.

Chapter 2

In his walk back to his office, Bob stopped abruptly and brought his thoughts back to the present. He had reached a side exit door to The Company, and he knew that on the other side of that door was the parking lot, and beyond that was the green grassy hillside he'd been gazing at from his office window. His office was just a little further down the hall from where he stood, along with all the work he should be doing. Hesitating, he glanced about furtively, but no one seemed to take any particular notice of him. As he thought again of the work waiting at his desk, he checked his watch. It was now nearly three thirty. With a heavy sigh he said quietly, "I'm tired and I don't want to do this anymore." Then he opened the door and exited the building.

The few people in the parking lot were intent on business of their own, so he put his hands in his pockets and walked nonchalantly through the parking lot and up the grassy hillside. As he walked he suddenly noticed something. At home he recently had been trying to launder his uniform as it seemed to be collecting a lot of gray smudges here and there. His attempts to clean the spots had been ineffective, and what he saw now was that his uniform was completely gray. He stopped for a moment and brushed at the sleeves as if to remove the gray, then shrugged and kept walking up the hill, allowing his thoughts to return to the day he'd been hired.

That day he was up earlier than usual. After a quick cup of coffee he showered and then stood contemplating his closet. He didn't own a business suit; his best shirt and slacks would have to do. But even as he studied the apparel in his closet, he knew the decision was not really so much about what to wear as it was about where he was headed. If he dressed intending to apply at The Company, and then backed out and went to work at the diner after all, his coworkers would want to know what was up with the fancy clothes. They might guess he was applying for a job elsewhere, and could even suspect he was being so arrogant as to apply to The Company. No, he couldn't go to work at the diner in anything but his usual jeans and uniform shirt. Taking a deep breath he chose the good slacks and slipped into them quickly before he could change his mind.

There was one more reason to be up earlier than usual, and that was that he didn't want to run into Sam on the way. A little heckling now and he just might back out after all. Even if Sam's joking was meant to be in fun, it wouldn't help his confidence, and right now he needed all the confidence he could muster.

He arrived at the front door to The Company in plenty of time to be ahead of Sam. As he stood there gathering up a last bit of courage, a man suddenly opened the door and exited in a huff. He was well-dressed in a black business suit and carrying a brief case. Although Bob didn't know for sure the reason for the man's presence, he looked like someone who just might successfully land a job at The Company. The man stopped short and looked Bob up and down for a moment before asking with a disdainful sniff, "If I'm not qualified, what *possible chance* do you think *you* have?"

Feeling slighted, Bob stared back at him hesitantly. *He's probably right. I should just forget about this, and get back home and change my clothes. Get on to work.* Somehow, a sense of determination rose up. Stubbornly he stuck out his chin and started to walk past the man toward the door. The man shook his head, and with a dismissive wave of his hand he walked away saying, "Don't waste your time. It's the craziest place I've ever seen anyway."

After watching the man walk away for an uneasy moment, Bob resolutely opened the door and slowly walked inside. He then stood still for a moment as he looked around at the reception area he had gazed at so many times through the windows. It was spacious, tidy and well furnished. Music played softly in the background. The peacefulness of the room made his nervousness seem out of place. Directing his attention toward the receptionist, he swallowed his apprehension and slowly approached her desk.

She was petite with curly white hair. Reading glasses perched on her nose. He guessed she was sixty-something, and reminded him of his own beloved grandmother. She was dressed again today in the spotless white uniform. A small gold name tag revealed that her name was Meredith. Bob cleared his throat before asking, "Uh – did you call me yesterday? What did you mean by, 'Turn around!'?"

She looked away from the computer screen and removed the glasses. Smiling pleasantly, she replied, "Well, you're here, aren't you?" Without waiting for a response, she added, "You're going to love The Manager." Then she giggled.

Bob was confused. *Is she amused, or just happy? And I sure don't have an appointment with The Manager!* He cleared his throat. "Oh, I don't have an appointment or anything. I just thought maybe I could pick up an application."

"Oh, an application," she said with a nod as her smile diminished. "Mm-hmm. So you think you're qualified to work here?" She opened a drawer and pulled out a packet of paper. She looked very serious and perhaps a bit concerned as she asked him, "You do understand a little about The Company – you know, that it's the very best there is? Really, it is completely unique and perfect."

Bob stood still for a moment, thinking hard. The confidence he had mustered was fading fast. "Well," he stammered, "I only thought about applying for an entry-level position. I'm not exactly – well, um, educated, you know, and I don't have any – uh, real experience."

"Hmm. The man you saw leaving as you came in had lots of education and lots of experience. He seemed to think he was absolutely qualified. But he wasn't quite perfect, now was he?"

She was smiling again, which only confused Bob further. What was she trying to tell him? The Company was perfect. The previous applicant was brimming over with qualifications. Yet, they had shown him the door. It was now likely time for him to just head for the door himself. He swallowed hard as he reminded himself that all he had to lose was pride. "Don't you have an application for – umm, just an entry-level position?"

Meredith was quite matter-of-fact as she handed him the papers with a flourish. "We only have one application. Everybody who works here only gets to fill out this application, no other. Requirements are the same for everybody, no matter what job they get."

It only took a glance at the first page to make Bob start to sweat. Not looking further, he tried to hand the application back, but the glasses had returned to their place on her nose, and her gaze was fixed on her computer monitor. "Well, I – uh…" he stammered. "I guess I'm really not qualified." He wondered if he had time now to get home to change into his jeans and get to the diner on time. *Bob, you're a dope! What a dumb idea this was!*

As the receptionist continued to ignore the application Bob was trying to hand back to her, a door behind her suddenly opened and a distinguished looking gentleman walked in. Standing tall and looking directly at Bob with a confident and friendly smile he said, "Welcome! I'm The Manager."

Bob felt shaky, but managed to squeak out as they shook hands, "I'm Bob. I was just – umm, leaving!"

As Bob stared at the man in amazement, he remembered the story he had heard long ago. He had scoffed when he first heard it, finding it nearly impossible to believe. The story was that this very man, The Manager, had come and lived among the people of the town. He seemed to be promoting The Company, and even inviting any and all who would listen to him to become a part of it. He had reportedly performed miraculous feats to prove the far-reaching power of The Company and its Ownership. Some claimed to be eye witnesses to such occurrences, but many others scoffed and even violently opposed the man.

Things had become volatile as most of the people disbelieved the man's descriptions of employment and even of life itself inside The Company. They hounded him with questions. "Who are you to tell us about life and The Company? How do we know you're really The Manager? Who are you to tell us how we should live?"

Eventually, the most prominent of the professors, the richest business owners and most influential of the community leaders formed a plot against him with the end result of his death at the hands of an angry mob.

And yet, the story wasn't over. After his death, there were rumors that his body had disappeared. Many said that his body had merely been stolen from the morgue by his followers, but some said the man had been raised back to life by The Owner of The Company, and he now resided permanently as The Manager of The Company.

To Bob these reports were the most unbelievable part of it all, and he had prided himself on not being gullible like so many. Over time, however, he had found himself wondering about it all, and finally coming to the conclusion that if there happened to be any truth to the story, he himself wanted to know and even be a part of it if possible. He had heard, however, that the standard of The Company was perfection and therefore unattainable, and as he stood there now he was sure it was true.

"Our application can be a little intimidating." The Manager spoke understandingly as Bob continued to stare at him incredulously. "Perhaps I can help." He reached over and took the papers Bob was still trying to hand to the receptionist. After glancing at them briefly, he looked up at Bob and asked, "Bob, do you think you measure up to these criteria?"

"No," Bob said weakly. He tried to think of some excuse as to why he was so very unqualified, but nothing came to mind. He should have seen this day coming long ago and somehow gotten ready for it. And now it was too late. He thought about the business-suited man who had just left. He had qualifications. And yet even he didn't get hired. So maybe it wouldn't have mattered even if Bob did have some sort of credentials to add to his name.

"Bob," The Manager said kindly, "You know, this is my Father's Company. He has put me directly in charge of all of it. I have authority over everything, including the hiring process. He did that because I put aside everything to do this for him. There is nothing I held back. I gave up everything for the sake of my Father and The Company. I gave up everything to be able to make this offer of employment to you."

Bob wasn't sure exactly what The Manager meant by all that; actually he didn't know why he was bothering to explain anything to him at all. There was a logical sequence that should be taking place at this moment. The Manager should be showing Bob the door while giving him a courteous speech: *"Thanks for showing interest in The Company. I regret that we are not able to offer you employment at this time."* Bob should nod politely, thank The Manager for his time, and race back home to change into his diner's uniform.

The Manager's feet did not head toward the door. Instead, he relaxed and leaned casually against Meredith's desk. "Bob, would you like to work for me, and for my Father? Would you like to become a part of The Company?"

For a moment Bob was speechless, but then he replied, "Yes." *How absurd! Surely now The Manager will laugh and show me the door.*

There was no laughter. Rather, The Manager looked pleased as he said, "Good! Bob, will you follow me to my office?" Not waiting for a response, he turned and left the room the same way he had come in, leaving the door open for Bob to follow. A bit stunned, Bob followed slowly at first, but then hurried to keep up. Shortly he found himself standing with The Manager in a spacious and pleasantly furnished office.

After asking Bob to take a seat, The Manager picked up a remote off his desk. "First of all, let's have a look at your previous employment at the diner, shall we?" A large screen behind The Manager's desk suddenly flickered to life, and Bob was shocked to see himself on the screen busy at his everyday duty of washing dishes at the diner. He nervously cleared his throat as the scene before him unfolded.

At first, Bob on screen appeared to be working hard as he scraped plates and loaded them into a dishwasher. Suddenly, however, he stopped and looked around as if to see if anyone happened to notice him. Then, after wiping his hands on his apron, he reached into a pocket and pulled out a cigarette and lighter. After puffing on the lit cigarette for a while, he walked over to a sign on the wall which plainly stated in large red letters, "No Smoking Allowed!" He blew a few smoke rings directly at the sign before depositing the cigarette butt into a half empty coffee cup on a tray of dirty dishes. Then he pulled out a cell phone and made a quick call to a friend, and then he used the phone to look up a favorite web site. When a waitress walked in to complain about the lack of clean dishes out front, he replied irritably, "Quit whining, they'll be out soon enough!"

The scene suddenly changed, and Bob continued to watch nervously as the on-screen Bob together with his friend Sam walked into a large walk-in refrigerator. Before long the two of them had devoured most of a cheesecake, definitely not an item on the list of employee meal choices.

Once again the scene changed, and Bob watched himself leave his apartment and start to walk down the street. Then he paused and made a phone call to his boss, feigning illness and saying he would not be in to work that day. After ending the call, he headed on down the street in a carefree manner. Soon he was in a video arcade, enthusiastically playing games and obviously not giving work another thought.

"Care to see more?" The Manager asked.

"Uh, no…" Bob stammered with a red face. "More" would only show himself behaving in a lazy and disrespectful manner to his boss and coworkers. More would show that he didn't care about the job, his boss, the people he worked with, nor even the customers of the diner. It would be all too obvious that if he had not been dependent on the paycheck he wouldn't have bothered to show up for work at all.

Bob stood slowly to his feet. It was quite clear that The Manager had no misconception about exactly who he was. Surely now would be a good time to thank him for his time and head quickly for the door. But his feet seemed stuck to the floor as thoughts kept spinning in his head. The Manager had seemed so kind. Had he really brought him into his office and shown him the video just to shame him?

The Manager's steady gaze revealed only sincerity as he said, "There is no way to be hired into The Company except through me. Bob, will you accept my offer of a position in The Company?"

Bob was stupefied. "I'm not sure I understand. Do you mean it? Because it's clear that you know everything about me. You know far more about me than just my lack of qualifications. You know I haven't been a good worker, and that I haven't been happy at work. You can see that I hate that job."

"Yes Bob, all these things I do know. But I assure you that my offer is sincere. I am giving you a chance to start over, to become new again. If you accept it with a willingness to change, then you will become an employee of The Company, just like that. All you have to do is say, "Yes," and trust me. Will you do that?"

As he hesitated momentarily, it occurred to Bob that all of his agonizing about what clothes to wear that morning had been completely unnecessary. He could have dressed as usual in his jeans and diner's shirt, even unlaundered with soils and stains, and walked in here to apply for a job, and the results right now would have been the same. It didn't matter what he had done or not done, it didn't matter how knowledgeable or ignorant he was, it didn't matter how trained or untrained, how skilled or unskilled he was. It certainly didn't matter what clothes he had on. He remembered the professionally dressed gentleman he had crossed paths with on his way in.

"You're wondering about the man who was leaving just as you arrived," The Manager said. "I gave him the same opportunity I am offering you. He turned it down. He couldn't believe the offer wasn't being made on the basis of his outstanding credentials and work history, you see. He felt his qualifications were quite impressive, and he was not willing to set all that aside to accept employment based solely on my grace. He wanted to believe he had earned it, that it was even his due, that in some way I owed him the opportunity. He also could not understand how I could or why I would make an offer not based on his own worthiness, and therefore he didn't trust me. It's important that you understand this offer is based completely on my good will, and no virtue nor accomplishments of your own. You have not earned it and you certainly don't deserve it. But I assure you, it is a completely sincere offer, and so I ask you once again. Will you trust me and accept my offer of a permanent position in The Company?"

Bob was sure the awestruck grin on his face looked a bit dopey, but he didn't care. With an overwhelming sense of gratitude and humility he replied, "Yes, Sir, I most thankfully accept your offer of employment, and I will trust you."

The Manager smiled and shook Bob's hand. "Welcome to The Company! My son, you have been lazy! However, you will be learning a new way to work, and you will find peace and fulfillment as you learn to trust me more each new day."

Although Bob knew he didn't completely understand everything The Manager was saying, he was happy beyond words, so he stood still and waited to see what would happen next.

The Manager's smile had changed a bit and he now looked almost mischievous. As Bob continued to stand still saying nothing he said, "We have not yet discussed compensation."

Bob stared back at him blankly for a moment. *Compensation?* It suddenly struck him. "Oh! You mean money!"

The Manager chuckled. "Yes. Money. You would like to be paid for working here, would you not?"

A bit sheepish, Bob stammered, "Well, yes, of course, uh, a paycheck would be, umm, important." He wondered why wages hadn't yet entered his mind, but then he realized that it didn't matter what the amount was, because there was no way he would reconsider and not take the offer after all.

"Any idea what your salary ought to be?"

How could he possibly know how to answer that? How could he determine even a rough estimate of compensation for a job which he was not qualified for, and in which he would have to be trained from the ground up? Maybe he should be the one to pay, just for the opportunity to work here!

When Bob remained speechless, The Manager said, "You know, Bob, money can't buy this gift of employment in The Company. It's far too valuable for that. It must be received as a free gift; it cannot be earned. Also, I want you to know that if money is your only motivation for working here, you will become dissatisfied and burn out quickly. So, having accepted my offer of employment, will you trust me that I will reward you for your work and I will supply all of your needs?"

"Yes Sir, I will." Still, Bob's thoughts were racing. *All of my needs? Wow, how can that be for one so unqualified in the first place? And what if I mess up – actually, how can I not mess up? I know absolutely nothing! Maybe I should be honest and ask about that right now!* "Sir, I don't have experience or training, so how will I know how to do the job, and what if I mess up?"

"Trust me, Bob, you will receive all the training you need. You are going to be learning new things every day. It will take time, but you will not be alone in your efforts. Some of what I want you to learn will come from Meredith and others like her. Some will come from the Employee Manual and other training materials. You will attend training classes and conferences. All of what you learn will come from me in one way or another. And Bob, when you fail, which you most assuredly will, I will help you get back on track. If you will keep on trusting me, I will walk you through all of it.

"Bob, there is one thing above all that you should always remember, and that is that I care very much for all of my employees. You will never have a problem that you and I together will not be able to work out. I will always be there for you, Bob. Do you understand?"

Bob hesitated. This was all too good to be true, and yet he knew he was hearing the truth. This man was sincere and straight forward and unlike any manager he had ever known before. Bob could sense that he truly did care. Finally he answered, "Yes, I understand. Well, at least I think I'm beginning to understand."

His old manager at the diner suddenly came to mind. *Won't he be surprised!* Uh – Sir, one more thing…" Bob spoke hesitantly.

"Yes, you're wondering about your old job, and giving them notice."

"Well, yes, it seems the right thing to do." Bob hoped his words would not somehow break the agreement.

The Manager smiled. "Yes, good, of course it is the right thing to do. Go ahead; call him right now to give him notice."

Bob pulled his cell phone from his pocket. He knew the number well, and dialed it automatically. He had dialed it frequently over the years, usually feigning illness or giving other lame excuses for not going in that day, but never to give notice. He felt a bit nervous, but also elated. In another moment he had his old boss on the line. "I have been offered a position by The Manager of The Company, so I won't need the job at your diner any more. I am giving you my notice."

"Well, if that's the way you are, just don't bother to come back at all!" The man was obviously angry, and ended the call without another word.

Bob stared at The Manager in bewilderment. "I guess he doesn't want any notice."

The Manager didn't seem at all surprised as he smiled and said, "Of course he doesn't. Now you are completely free to work for me!"

Chapter 3

Bob had reached the top of the grassy hill. Turning around, he looked back down at The Company building. He thought of the work assignments waiting at his desk, and the people who would be disappointed if he failed to do his part. Shrugging off those thoughts, he turned his gaze to the other side of the hill. The grass and trees made a pretty scene, and seemed to invite him to continue on. Again, he heard the song of the meadowlark and tried to locate it. There it was, perched on a fence not far away. He watched it for a few moments before walking just far enough down the hill that he wouldn't be visible from even the top floor of The Company building.

Choosing a spot on the lush green grass, he sat down and looked again at his gray uniform. The significance of it was not lost on him. Although at first he had paid little attention to the color of uniforms, he had gradually come to realize that it was actually an indication of an employee's work habits and attitudes. The longer one strayed from diligence, the more smudged and gray his uniform became. Completely gray meant an increasingly unenthusiastic employee had finally gone completely over the edge of indolence.

Bob remembered when he used to try to avoid employees that didn't share his enthusiasm for the work place. Lately however, the ones he avoided were those whose uniforms were spotlessly white. *Well, what do they know? Maybe they don't have the problems with work that I have. Maybe all of their emails and phone calls are responded to quickly with exactly what they need to carry on with a project. Maybe they don't have an overwhelming amount of work to do in the first place. Maybe they don't have a Charlie telling them what to do and how to do it all the time. Maybe they are constantly given praise and appreciation for the work they do. Maybe,*

maybe, maybe…

The realization that he had finally succumbed to the mind-set of the rebellious gave Bob an uneasy and guilty feeling. *How have I managed to stray so far? If I told The Manager I was having problems, would he not help me somehow? If I told him I needed a specific resource, wouldn't he see that I got it so I could get my work done? If I told him in a respectful manner that I was having problems with Charlie, would he not somehow help me even with that? Well, I don't care. I'm tired. This is hard and it isn't fair. And I don't even want to think about just how hard I might have to work to get back to where I used to be.*

With a shake of his head, he tried to dismiss all thoughts of work along with his sense of guilt. It was pleasant out here in the sunshine. Birds chirped happily from the trees, and the meadowlark called again and again from its perch atop the fence. A butterfly floated by on the warm, gentle breeze, lazily seeking flowers. Breathing in the fresh air, Bob tried to relax and simply enjoy the peaceful surroundings, but the memories of the day he had been hired intruded upon his thoughts once again.

He remembered that The Manager had assigned Meredith to get him outfitted with a new white uniform, give him a brief tour of The Company, and take him to HR to complete his new employee paper work. First, she took him to a fitness facility that included a workout gym, a pool, and a basketball court. There was also a room there with racks of spotless white employee uniforms. Finding one in his size, she handed it to him and pointed out the men's locker room where he could change.

When he was ready, she escorted him around the building, pointing out the different departments and explaining some essential facts about them, as well as the layout of the building and where to find simple things like stairs and elevators, as well as the employee break room. Then she showed him where his office would be. Workers were already there, getting it set up for him at The Manager's direction. The rest of the morning he spent in HR filling out the required new employee paperwork and looking over the Employee Handbook and other work related pamphlets. It was an overwhelming amount of information, but knowing he didn't have to absorb it all at once gave him a certain sense of peace and freedom. What gave him the biggest sense of relief, however, was that he did not have to fill out an application, and there would be no background check. The Manager knew it all, and yet he was accepted.

The time flew, and suddenly it was approaching noon and time for lunch. Meredith led the way to the cafeteria which was already crowded. People were either getting a tray filled or were already seated and eating while chatting with coworkers. Just standing in the food line was exciting – everything looked and smelled so good. There were so many different choices that it was hard to decide what to have. He thought about what he might be having if he were at the diner today. Grilled cheese or tuna fish, maybe a hamburger. He began to salivate as he stared at the roast baron of beef being carved by a cafeteria worker.

Suddenly he became aware that Meredith had turned away from looking at the food choices and was staring at him intently. "Are you hungry?" she asked when she saw she had his attention.

"Yeah, starving!" He glanced eagerly at the enticing array of food.

"Okay, come on." Putting aside her tray, she turned and started for the back of the room.

"Wait, where are you going?"

"Well, you did say you were hungry, didn't you?" Meredith stopped and stared at him as if he were being unreasonable.

"Well, sure I'm hungry, but what's wrong with all this food? It looks really good to me!" He looked toward the back of the room where there was nothing more than a simple vending machine. It looked so plain and colorless that Bob wasn't sure it actually was a normal vending machine at all. Even from this distance he could see that it didn't hold the chips, soda pop and candy bars that any normal vending machine would have. It surely couldn't offer the wide variety of meats and cheeses, casseroles, salads, breads and desserts he was trying to choose from in the cafeteria line. Raising an eyebrow at her, he said, "Meredith, it doesn't look to me like there is a lot of food back there in that vending machine!"

Meredith sighed in exasperation. "All right, we'll eat off the line today. But this will only satisfy you temporarily, Buster, trust me!"

That was the first but far from the last time Meredith called him 'Buster.' He rather liked it because he could tell she wasn't really angry, and that she liked him. Although he found her resolute manner amusing, he was growing in respect for her at the same time. He wondered what she meant exactly, that the food would only satisfy him temporarily, but he decided to ignore the comment and get back to making his selections.

Once they had filled their trays, they sat at a table with a few other employees. Meredith and the others chatted easily like old friends, but they were also welcoming toward Bob and asked a few questions to include him in the conversation. Although he felt a bit embarrassed to admit his only recent work experience was bussing tables and washing dishes at the diner, they remained friendly and non-judgmental. In fact, as his new coworkers shared their own histories, he quickly realized that most of them had undistinguished backgrounds similar to his own. He remembered that The Manager had told him no one was hired into The Company based on their own merit. He also realized that in spite of their own unremarkable pasts, they all seemed confident of their place in The Company. He only hoped he could become as confident in his own new position.

The food tasted every bit as good as it looked, and it didn't take Bob long to finish off every bite. As they were finishing up, Meredith received a phone call to let them know Bob's office was ready, so she sent him off to check it out on his own, saying they would get together again in a while.

When he got to his office Bob took a moment to quietly survey the tiny room. *My own office, is this for real?* He had never even had his very own desk in any work environment, let alone his own office. A computer monitor and keyboard took up much of the desk surface. He opened a few drawers and saw that they contained everything he might need down to pencils and erasers. Neat stacks of copy paper sat by the printer. File cabinets lined a wall. He couldn't even guess what they might contain. He felt an almost silly sense of delight in everything down to the smallest item, even a stapler sitting on the desk.

He found the computer stored out of sight in a bottom cabinet of the desk. His experience with computers was fairly limited, so he couldn't help but feel a bit apprehensive as he wondered how he would be using this one in his new job. Still, The Manager had told him not to worry and assured him there would be plenty of training, so he let his anxious thoughts dissipate and focused instead on his incredible good fortune. He thought about it in amazement throughout that first day, and wondered how long it would take for his sense of elation to diminish. Thoughts of his former job came to him briefly, but mainly with a sense of relief to finally have it in the past.

When he rejoined Meredith, he asked a few questions, and then together they went to his office again where she spent some time helping him to become familiar with the basics of his computer. Then once again she left him alone to spend some time reading the Employee Manual. Before he knew it the day was nearly over; it was almost time to go home. That's when Meredith showed up at his office door and announced, "One more thing before you leave for the day! It's time for cake!"

"Cake? What are we celebrating?"

"You, of course!"

"Me?" Bob's eyebrows rose in surprise. She didn't wait to explain, however, and he hurried to catch up with her as she led the way down the hall. It occurred to him that in spite of her age, she was quite lively and spirited. He wondered if she had always been that way, or if she was energized because she was so happy to be working for The Company.

Shortly they entered a conference room which was already crowded with employees holding coffee or other assorted drinks as they stood in small groups, talking and laughing. In the center of the room was a table with a large cake waiting to be cut. A woman in a chef's apron stood back to survey her work. She had just finished decorating the cake with colorful balloons and the words, "Welcome, Bob!" in large letters.

"Gosh," Bob spoke quietly to Meredith, "I get cake on my first day? Usually a person gets cake when he leaves a company, not when he starts."

"Well now, leaving's nothing to celebrate is it? If you leave, that's a sad thing!" Meredith smiled at him quizzically as though wondering exactly what it was about cake on his first day that he couldn't understand. "This is a day for rejoicing, just because you've joined us! We're happy to have you here and we want you to know that!"

Her enthusiasm was contagious, and Bob found himself laughing slightly. He glanced around the room at his new coworkers a bit nervously as Meredith made an announcement. "Listen, everybody! This is Bob, our newest employee, just starting today. Please join me in welcoming him to The Company!"

There was a spirited round of applause in response. "Welcome, Bob," a few voices called out. Bob smiled and nodded in return, hoping his nervousness wasn't too obvious.

The Manager himself then entered the room and joined in on the festive occasion, taking the opportunity to introduce Bob individually to a few of the employees. There were strong handshakes, a few light slaps on the back, and even a light hug or two. They chatted casually between bites of cake washed down with coffee. Everyone smiled and eye contact was direct and sincere. In fact, if they held him in any sort of low regard, they didn't show it. His amazement was growing at the unconditional acceptance he felt from not only The Manager, but everyone he met. This was so unexpected.

As he thought about it, he realized that one of the main things that had always held him back from applying for employment in The Company was his fear of what the other employees within The Company might think of him. *I don't think I would have been so worried about all that if I had just realized that the basis for employment in The Company is the same for all, and that is the grace and word of The Manager.*

Chapter 4

Still sitting on the grass, Bob pulled out his phone and glanced at the time. *4pm? How can it be getting so late? I really should get back inside and get some work done. Nah. It's nice out here. If I go back inside the first thing I'd have to do is read Charlie's email. Not gonna happen. Not right now. Tomorrow's soon enough.*

His thoughts drifted into the past again.

The first few days in The Company passed quickly. Although there were so many new things to learn, Bob sensed an incomparable value in the learning process. He also recognized a change deep inside himself that was being fueled not only by the training and education he was receiving, but by the encouragement and helpfulness of his coworkers and especially The Manager himself. Old attitudes of rebellion and feelings of inadequacy and despair were being replaced with a new sense of willingness, courage and optimism he had never experienced before.

Something he hadn't even thought about was soon upon him though, and that was a day off from work. Days off from the diner had been a huge relief, even if he didn't really do anything special with them. Simply not having to be at or even think about a job he hated was a welcome break. Now in The Company, however, he looked forward to work days with enthusiasm, not dread, and he even felt he was having way more fun than anyone ought to have at work. In so many ways it was more like an adventure than a mere job. He was also becoming sincerely fond of his coworkers, and regretted that he wouldn't be spending time with them that day. Most of all, he realized he would miss his early morning routine of coffee with The Manager. It was natural therefore that his first thoughts on awakening that morning had not been about what to do with his day off, but rather about all that had been going on at work. He had been so focused on his assignments that it didn't seem logical to take time away from pursuing them.

Well, no matter, today he was on his own and he had to decide how to spend the time. That was when he realized he hadn't seen his old friends since he'd left the diner. *Maybe I should just drop in and say hello.* And so he dressed, gulped down some coffee and a piece of toast, and headed for the diner. He whistled cheerfully on the way, thinking as he walked of everything he would tell his former coworkers. He remembered the times of joking and even outright ridicule against The Company he had participated in with them. Well, now he knew better. He looked forward to sharing the truth with them, and imagined how glad they would be to hear all about it.

Just as before, his route to the diner took him by The Company. Unable to resist, he stopped and peeked through the window just as he had so many times before. Remembering the sense of hopeless yearning he had felt before just by looking through the window, he chuckled. *This is so totally amazing that I still can't believe it's true. I'm working in the very company I've always thought to be the impossible dream!* He had planned to walk on by, but after watching Meredith at her desk for a moment, he suddenly found himself going inside.

"What are you doing here?" Meredith quizzed him with a welcoming smile. "Don't you know a day off is a good thing?"

He grinned a bit sheepishly. "Yeah, I suppose it is. Just missed your smiling face I guess."

Meredith smiled back affectionately. "Of course you did! The Manager gave me a message for you."

"He did? He knew I'd stop by?"

Meredith didn't answer his questions, but said simply, "Wherever you go, I am."

Bob blinked. "That's the message?"

"Mmhmm. That's it. Now get out of here and go have some fun!" She sounded like a mother telling her kids to go outside and play.

"Okay, I will try to have fun! You have a great day, Meredith!" He left feeling glad he had stopped in, but wondered just what The Manager had meant by, "Wherever you go, I am."

When he reached the diner he hesitated. Doubts had begun to edge their way into his confidence. What would they all really think of him now? Would they be as happy to hear the truth as he had imagined? Maybe he should just go home. "Stop being stupid," he scolded himself. He straightened his shirt and took a deep breath before opening the door and stepping inside.

The first person he saw was the hostess standing by to greet customers. "Hey, Deborah, how are you?" he asked with a friendly smile.

Deborah seemed at first a bit surprised to see him, but then shrugged indifferently. She frowned slightly as she looked him up and down. Then she replied, "I'm okay, Bob. How are you? Oh – will you excuse me? I have to help Mike serve coffee. We're a bit busy around here today, you know." Her attitude suggested he should have known better than to stop by unannounced. She walked away and grabbed a coffee carafe. Unsmiling, she gave him only a glance or two as she moved about the room pouring refills into customers' cups.

The Mike she spoke of was waiting tables, and gave only a slight nod in Bob's direction. Nancy, a waitress, was the only one who stopped for a moment and walked deliberately over to Bob. He wished she hadn't as she said with a smirk, "Well, taking a little time to come back and gloat? Or, have you already been fired from your fancy new job?" With a mocking laugh she turned away and went back to waiting on tables.

Nancy had never been particularly friendly, always negative and complaining about something, so Bob knew he shouldn't pay her too much mind. Still, her words stung. He hoped Sam at least would be glad to see his old friend. He hesitated at the doorway into the kitchen. Asking for permission to go back there was probably the appropriate thing to do now that he no longer worked there, but a glance around the diner confirmed that all employees were ignoring him, most likely intentionally, so he pushed the door open and walked through it.

Bob noted with some surprise that someone other than Sam was at the grill, and Sam was washing dishes. He hoped his resignation had not in some way caused a demotion for him.

As Sam looked up from the dishes, he didn't look particularly surprised to see Bob. With a slight nod he asked simply, "How are ya?"

"I'm great!" Somehow even to himself, his words sounded overly enthusiastic. Toning it down a bit, he asked, "How about you?"

"So-so. Busy." Sam didn't smile, and Bob felt a strange tension between them. After another moment of banging around the pots and pans he was scrubbing, Sam pointed to a vacant chair. "Sit a minute. Let me finish up, then we'll go for a walk."

Bob sat and watched him finish his chores, and soon they were headed out the door together. "Sam, why aren't you at the grill? I'm sure you didn't ask for my old job as dishwasher!"

"Yeah, like I'd do that! Nah, the boss had an opportunity to hire a fry cook, and you'd left us high and dry without a dishwasher, so there we go. He assures me it's only temporary; soon as he can get someone in there to wash dishes I'm back to workin' the grill."

Chatting casually about some other insignificant changes at the diner, they headed toward a nearby coffee house they used to frequent. They hadn't gotten past a few sips of coffee and bites of pastry though before casual conversation began to stall. Their old style of banter was missing, and The Company loomed between them, yet neither seemed to know what to say. Finally Bob cleared his throat and began, "You know, Sam, we were all wrong about The Company. It's really a great place to work. It's The Manager – he honestly seems to care about everyone. He's wonderful, and so is The Company…" His voice trailed off as he saw the look of exasperation spread across Sam's face.

Pushing aside his half-eaten pastry, Sam lit up a cigarette. After a long draw on it he looked at Bob with a disapproving frown and said, "Bob, I don't mean to be rude, but I really don't wanna hear about The Company from you! I know you too well. You and I, we're pretty much the same. We worked together at the same old diner for years. We hung out at the same bars and got into trouble together, you and me. You're no different from me. So, now you got this great fancy job at The Company, and you think you're some kinda hot shot. Well, you can think what you want, but don't tell me all about how great you have it now at The Company."

Dismayed, Bob shook his head in protest. "Sam, it's not like that. I don't think…"

Sam interrupted, "I don't give a rip. You got that? I'm leavin' now before they kick me out for lightin' up a cig. Gotta get back to work anyway." Standing up, he said with an air of artificial politeness, "Nice to see you again." With that he walked out, leaving Bob sitting alone in stunned silence.

After a few minutes of gloomy reflection, Bob left the coffee house as well. Wandering aimlessly through the downtown area, he stopped now and then to stare at the merchandise in some of the shop display windows, but he really hardly even saw what he was looking at. His mind was on the words of his former coworkers, especially the things Sam had said. *Maybe he was right; we are pretty much the same. Maybe I am in The Company under some sort of false pretense.*

He shook off the thought. He hadn't lied about his qualifications. Everyone, especially The Manager himself, all knew he had come into The Company on the basis of the grace and word of The Manager, not on any merit of his own. It was a gift, and he knew he had been given an amazing opportunity. Why couldn't his former coworkers understand that?

As he stood staring vacantly at a large painting in an art shop, he suddenly became aware that someone had stopped and was standing beside him and looking at the painting too. He turned slightly and nodded a simple acknowledgement toward the man, intending to continue his aimless walk, but the man spoke. "You know, this painting's okay, but it's a bit overpriced, don't you think?"

Bob looked back at the painting, this time examining it carefully, and then he looked at the price tag. "Yeah," he agreed with a chuckle. "I sure wouldn't pay that for it!" He sensed that the man didn't really care about the price of paintings, though, and was probably just looking for someone to talk to.

As if to confirm Bob's thoughts, the man asked, "So, young man, what brings you out on this nice day?"

"Day off from work. Nothing really to do, just wandering."

"Me too. I hate work, but at least it gives me something to do. I work right down the block at Newman's Department Store. I've been there going on twenty years now! How about you, young man, where do you work?"

Bob thought before responding. His last conversation about The Company hadn't gone well at all. Maybe he shouldn't even mention it. He remembered suddenly Meredith's message to him from The Manager. "Wherever you go, I am." What did that mean? Although he wasn't exactly sure, an overwhelming desire to please The Manager rose in him as he contemplated once again how amazing it was to be in the employ of The Company. Smiling sincerely he replied to the man, "I work at The Company. Only just got hired a week ago."

The man looked thoughtful yet sad for a moment before he answered, "Oh. Well, I've sometimes thought about trying to work for The Company. Thing is, I'm just a store clerk, and I don't have the most exemplary work history at that. I can't see what they'd want with a guy like me, know what I mean?"

Bob nodded enthusiastically and exclaimed, "I do know exactly what you mean! I didn't really think they'd want me either, but the thing I found out is The Manager is amazing, and he wants to give people the opportunity, and your qualifications don't matter at all. I worked at the diner on the corner down there! I was a dishwasher, but look at me now! I'm an employee of The Company!" Bob was surprised at the fervor in his own voice.

The man didn't seem offended by Bob's eagerness, but he did look skeptical. "Really? No background training? No other job you did before that would have gotten your foot in the door?"

"I know it's hard to believe, but I had no training or experience whatsoever. I was so completely unqualified that I am still amazed The Manager gave me this chance! When he hired me, The Manager told me no one gets hired on the basis of their own merit." Bob thought seriously for a moment, and then he asked, "So, you know the story – how The Manager came to live in the town, and how he was killed by that mob, and then was raised back to life by his Father, the Owner of The Company?"

The man replied, "Yeah, I sure know the story!"

"Well, the thing is, I didn't know what to believe for a long time about that, but now I believe that it really is all true! And I'm beginning to understand that he allowed that all to happen somehow for our sake, to rescue us. It's the reason he can hire us although we are not worthy! It's like he traded his worthiness for our unworthiness!"

The man stared at Bob for a long moment before asking hesitantly, "Then you think maybe The Manager would give me a chance, too?"

"Yes, I do, absolutely! I'm going back there right now, you can come with me and we'll go inside together if you'd like!"

"Well, I'm not really dressed for an interview…"

"Trust me, it doesn't matter!"

Together they walked to The Company, chatting casually on the way. Bob found out that his name was Edward, and that he had a wife and a couple of kids. Although his family life was currently riddled with problems, Bob had the sense that if the man became an employee of The Company, things would be better for him and his family as well.

It was a short walk, and in no time, the man had gone into the back offices with The Manager, leaving Bob standing with Meredith once again. Mischievously, she asked, "So this is how you spend your time off, recruiting new hires for The Company?"

Bob smiled back and shrugged. "I guess what you said – the message from The Manager – was right. I don't think running into this man was an accident. He seems as ready to become an employee as I was."

"Yes, he surely does! And how are things at the diner?" When Bob's smile quickly faded, her own expression changed to one of sympathy. "Oh, sweetie! Did you think they'd roll out the red carpet for you? You're not one of them any more, you know."

Bob smiled again and leaned forward on her desk, resisting an urge to hug her. "How do you always know everything, Meredith? I didn't tell anybody I was visiting the diner today." As he spoke, he looked at her sweet, motherly face, seeing only the sincere kindness of a caring friend. What a contrast to the animosity he had faced earlier! His pain began to dissipate.

Now as Bob sat on the grassy hillside, he felt troubled by the memory of that day. Helping that man find his way into The Company had given him a sense of fulfillment he'd never experienced before. He had been so happy then, how had he managed to become so wretchedly hopeless? How had he gotten here, sitting outside and wondering where to go and what to do? Once again he glanced around and let the warm sunshine soak into him. *This feels good. Maybe I can just stay here and listen to the birds and watch the butterflies. I can't keep working like I have been. It's too hard. I'm too tired.*

He thought about what Mark had just said in the break room, that he was thinking about quitting and returning to his old job because it was less stressful and less difficult. *How exactly the way I'm feeling right now! I'm tired. I don't want to do this any more. Back at the diner I wouldn't have all this stress! I don't want to go back to the diner, but maybe I should. Maybe that's where I belong after all.* There didn't seem to be any answers, and he was tired of thinking about it. Moving from a sitting position to lying down on his stomach, he flattened down a patch of grass for his face. Drowsiness took over completely and in a few moments he had fallen sound asleep.

Chapter 5

Bob was rousing slowly from sleep. Something didn't feel right. He felt chilled, and a cold breeze ruffled his hair. Struggling to open his eyes, he slowly lifted his head from the ground. When he managed to look around, he gasped. The sky was dark and heavy with storm clouds. *What happened to the warm sunshine? Where are the chirping birds?* He rubbed his eyes and looked around again, but the clouds were still there and the chilly breeze was rapidly changing to a cold, gusty wind. *Relax, calm down! It's just a storm and it's going to rain, that's all.*

Groggily he pushed himself to his feet and walked slowly to the top of the hill. His feet felt heavy and sluggish, making every step a concentrated effort. As he walked he noticed in bewilderment that the green grassy hillside he'd fallen asleep on was now lifeless and brown. *It's still summer – isn't it? I only took a short nap – didn't I?*

When he reached the top of the hill, he stopped and stared in bewilderment at the scene below. The parking lot at the base of the hill was nearly empty, and the few cars that did remain looked old and broken down. Some of the car windows were shattered and the glass was strewn about the pavement. Dry leaves, dirt and discarded paper swirled about in the cold wind, and some of it had settled against flat tires.

A deep sense of remorse and dread settled over him as he looked past the parking lot and stared at the building itself. The side door he had exited through seemingly only a few minutes ago now stood open and hanging half off its hinges, allowing the swirling wind to blow trash and dirt right into the building. *What has happened? What on earth is going on?*

He began to shiver, and wondered if it was just because of the cold wind, or due more to the frightening scene before him.

Forgetting grogginess and heavy feet, he ran down the hill, not stopping until he reached the building. Brushing aside some old and dirty cobwebs which clung to the door frame, he took a deep breath and gingerly stepped inside. *I have to get to my office – I have to finish all my incomplete assignments! I'll stop at the break room and get coffee first and I'll work all night if I have to.*

Even as the thoughts registered, he realized how absurd they were. He had failed, and with that knowledge came a heavy sense of guilt and fear. *How could I have been so stupid as to abandon my work? Any efforts now will surely be in vain! It can't be in vain, I have to get the work done!*

He stared first one way and then the other down the hallways which were normally well-lit and bustling with coworkers. Now all was dark and nearly deserted, but Bob could make out a few shadowy figures. He quickly realized that most of them were the dark-hooded demons. Normally either completely invisible or lurking about stealthily like shadowy illusions, they now appeared openly, fearlessly, and seemed to move about with an eerie but calm determination. Whatever their evil business none bothered to approach him, a fact he recognized with relief and yet with some unease. *Do they ignore me because they know somehow they've already won and there's nothing I can do against them now?* Giving them a wide berth, he forgot about coffee and the break room and hastened toward his office.

As he walked, he also saw a few coworkers in gray uniforms, but they looked just as confused as he felt. They were mostly just standing still and scratching their heads as if in disbelief. *Had they been napping, too?* He discarded thoughts of speaking to them as useless; they probably didn't know any more than he did. As he walked, he tried to reason away his fears. *Maybe it isn't too late. Why should the demons care about anything in my office? Maybe at least there, all will be fine.*

His forced optimism was crushed as he arrived at his office door and looked inside. Far from having escaped the destructive behavior of the demons, it looked like a tornado had passed through. Even now the demons were still at their evil task of tossing files about and tearing up papers. Bob's torn and crumpled work projects littered the floor. His computer monitor was also on the floor, the screen broken. The desk phone was off the hook, beeping incessantly, and his desk lamp was overturned.

One of the dark-cloaked demons sat down on Bob's desk and slowly turned an evil gaze toward him. Slowly and ominously with a deep gravelly voice, the demon spoke. "You thought you could take a little nap and wake up to find everything still in order. What a fool you are!" The pronouncement was followed by hideous laughter.

Frozen in terror and disbelief, Bob stared silently, helplessly. *This can't be happening. Why, oh why, did I go outside and fall asleep on the grass? I should have been more careful! If I had stayed and kept on working, surely all this wouldn't be happening!* The thoughts ran through his head wildly even as he stared at the devastation and its perpetrators.

The other demons stopped their destructive behavior and glared maliciously at him. One of them snarled, "You *sleep?* When there is so much work to do, you *sleep?* You are a lazy fool! You were never good enough to work here anyway, and now you've proven it!"

"Too tired to finish anything, aren't you? Need a little slumber, huh?" one of the others mocked him. "You know this work was too hard for you! You're no good at this or anything else for that matter!"

"Yeah, you're no good!" another chimed in. "Why don't you just *give up* and go on back to the diner where *you belong?* Maybe you can still wash dishes if you're lucky!"

They all laughed hideously and started chanting, "Give up! Go back to the diner! You're no good! Go back to the diner! Give up! Give up!" Their laughter and pointed accusations pierced Bob's mind and heart like daggers. He briefly considered that they were right. *I have been a fool. I was given the opportunity of a lifetime, and I wasted it.*

He didn't have time to let the consequences of his actions sink in further. Even now the demons were approaching him stealthily. Somehow they looked not just evil, but hungry, as if the havoc and destruction they had already caused were not enough. Backing away in fear and revulsion, Bob turned and ran down the hall with the sound of their vile laughter echoing behind him. *This just can't be happening. Where is everybody?*

He thought of Meredith, the one who was always there and always seemed to have answers to problems. *Surely, somehow she can help me now.* With a sudden burst of hopefulness, he ran toward the reception area and her desk. *Surely the lobby at least will be normal, peaceful and quiet.* He couldn't picture it any other way.

When he reached the lobby he halted abruptly and stared with anguished disappointment. Meredith's desk and the reception area were as dark as the rest of the building. There was no soft music playing. Meredith herself was nowhere to be seen. Her computer and monitor were smashed onto the floor, and trash littered the area. "Meredith, Meredith!" His cries of despair went unanswered.

He turned away hopelessly. Then he remembered The Door. In a state of complete panic, he broke into a desperate run. As he turned into the hallway that led to The Door, he realized it was as dimly lit as the rest of the building. He slowed to a walk, approaching apprehensively. As he feared, the destruction was extensive. The file cabinet drawers were mostly open; some drawers were even out of the cabinets and on the floor in disarray, and the project papers themselves were strewn about like piles of discarded rubbish.

Turning his attention to the once beautiful golden door, he saw it was now dingy gray and covered in cobwebs. But worst of all, it was closed with not even a small ray of light shining through. Bob had always seen it standing open, and had never even imagined it closed. Hastening through the chaotic mess of overturned boxes, he reached the Door and tried to push it open. It wouldn't budge. There was no handle. *Had there ever been a handle? Why can't I remember if it had a handle?*

With a miserable sigh, he turned away from the Door and rummaged through the paper projects until he found some of his own. Like the others, they were torn and gritty with dust, and it was quite obvious no one had touched them in some time. Nowhere was there a single sign that anyone cared about any of it any more.

Thoughts of The Manager himself suddenly gripped Bob. *Where is The Manager? Has he already gone through the door, closing it behind him forever?* There was one more place he had to go, and that was the Executive Offices. He turned slowly and headed out into the hallway again. He walked slowly with his head down, thinking hard. *If he's there, what will he say to me? I've completely blown it. What will he think of me? Will he accept any of my excuses? How angry will he be? Will he fire me?*

Suddenly he found he had reached a wall. That was odd; he didn't remember this hallway coming to an end like that. Somehow he must have gotten into the wrong hallway. Turning around, he walked back until he reached a corner, and turned down another hallway. Soon however, he found himself staring at another wall. He didn't remember any of the halls in The Company having dead ends like that. Any hallway that did reach the end of the building had a window in the end wall, and you could always look out and see exactly where you were. Once again he turned back and walked until he reached yet another intersection of darkened hallways. He stood still and wondered bleakly which way to go this time. *Why don't the hallways look familiar? Where is the one to The Manager's office?*

He finally chose a hall and began slowly walking again. This time he noticed some things he hadn't noticed before. There were no open office doors. All the doors were exactly the same. Where was even a break room, or a restroom for that matter? Stopping, he gingerly tried to open one of the doors. No luck, it was apparently locked.

He looked around, finally realizing that he was completely alone. Not another befuddled employee was in sight, and he didn't even see a demon. Stubbornly, he kept walking. For a long while he seemed to be entering one unfamiliar hallway after another, and none of them led anywhere, and The Manager's office was nowhere in sight. He couldn't even find his own office or the reception area. At last he stopped and stood still, realizing fearfully that he was hopelessly trapped in a dark and dreary endless maze without so much as a doorway to the outside of the building.

A cold wind suddenly enveloped him. Startled, he fell backward onto the floor as a demon towered over him. With cruel eyes staring intently at Bob, the demon's words were abrupt. "You are a worthless creature, and you are fired!" Then it turned and glided silently away.

Although he wasn't sure the demon had any authority to actually fire him in the first place, it was obvious there was nowhere to go, there were no options to pursue, and worst of all The Manager could not be found. *This is it! I'm out!* Bob's despair was complete. Bowing to the floor, he covered his face and began to weep in sorrow and hopelessness.

Chapter 6

"Wake up, wake up!" From somewhere inside his groggy half-consciousness Bob heard the voice calling. Awakening with a disoriented start, he pushed himself to a sitting position and looked around in a dazed stupor. He was no longer weeping alone on the floor of a dark hallway, but was back on the grassy hillside where he had decided to take a nap. He blinked a few times, rubbed his eyes and brushed a few bits of grass from his face and shirt. A warm breeze ruffled his hair. Fluffy white clouds were scattered across a pale blue sky. Birds sang and nearby a butterfly flitted among flowers. *Was it just a bad dream, a horrible nightmare?*

He heard the voice calling out again, "Wake up! Wake up!" He suddenly realized the voice was Meredith's. Now fully awake, he jumped to his feet and hastened to the top of the hill.

He reached the crest of the hill just in time to see Meredith going back into the building through the same side door he had exited through. He stood still and stared at The Company. Everything looked just as it had before his nightmare. The parking lot was full of neatly parked cars. There was no trash and broken glass littering the pavement. People came and went through the fully functioning side door. It was too good to be true, but everything was just as he had left it. He glanced at his phone to see just how long his little nap had taken. How odd, it had only been a few minutes. The nightmare had seemed unending.

Breathing a shaky sigh of relief, he headed down the hill and across the parking lot. As he entered the building, he paused for a moment and looked around. The sight of employees bustling about in routine activity was reassuring, but then he remembered Meredith calling, "Wake up, wake up!" *So Meredith knows I was sleeping. Does The Manager know? If he doesn't know, should I be up front and admit to it? What will happen if I do? Will The Manager fire me?*

Bob's thoughts were racing as he stood there, but he took a deep breath to calm himself. *Don't be a dope! It was just a nightmare, nothing more than a bad dream, and everything's okay, just as you left it.* He continued to stand motionless, willing his uneasy thoughts to be still. *Maybe it wouldn't hurt to just check in with Meredith.* He turned and went to her reception desk in the front office. Once there he stopped and surveyed the room. All was normal, and the background music was soothing. He took a moment to pull himself together before approaching her desk and asking calmly, "Hey, Meredith. Did you call me? Did you call out for me to wake up?"

Meredith stopped clicking the keys on her keyboard and slid her glasses down to perch on the end of her nose. Peering at Bob over the lenses with a slight frown she asked tersely, "Well, you were sleeping, weren't you?"

Bob blinked innocently before answering with an indifferent shrug, "Yeah, I – uh – I guess I was taking a bit of a nap."

"Hmm. So it seems." Meredith took the glasses off and sat back in her chair, studying him with a soul piercing scrutiny.

Bob looked back coolly as though napping were part of a normal work day. "I was a little tired, no big deal. So, I guess I should get back to work now!" Her only response was to raise her eyebrows slightly before putting her glasses back on and returning to her computer.

Back in his office, Bob was relieved to see that nothing looked out of the ordinary. There were no torn and crumpled files littering the floor. His computer looked perfectly undamaged. The phone sat in its cradle with no incessant beeping. *Apparently, the sky's not falling and demons aren't lurking around every corner after all.* He stared out the window and listened for a moment to the meadowlarks before sitting down at his desk.

Still reflecting on the dream, he sat motionless for a minute. It may have been only a dream, but he felt unsettled and had questions with no answers. *Only a dream yet too real, a warning possibly, of just how far I have strayed. Still, what can I do? Well, for one thing I can get to work and try to actually accomplish something around here! What a lazy slug I've been!*

He remembered the email from Charlie he had deleted earlier, the one titled, 'AS SOON AS YOU GET THIS.' *I probably should have read it right away; I'd certainly better read it now.* He opened his email program and then the trash folder to retrieve Charlie's email he had deleted, but then he quickly sat back in alarm. Not only was that email not in the trash folder, but the entire folder was empty! He certainly hadn't emptied it himself, and it wasn't set to empty automatically.

Anxiously he quickly opened his inbox. Enough time had elapsed that there should have been several new work related emails. He stared in bewilderment as he saw there were no new messages, and most of the old ones had apparently been deleted. Whoever had done that must have then emptied the trash folder as well. *Why would anyone do such a thing? Bob, you are in big trouble. What on earth is going on here? Maybe it's just a glitch. Maybe everybody's missing emails. Maybe it'll be fixed soon by IT. Just get some work done, anything!*

Resolutely he opened his computer documents and began looking for a particular file he'd been working on earlier. It was part of the critically important project he'd been working on earlier, and had a deadline looming. He didn't relish the prospect of working on it at all, but the impending deadline gave him a sense of urgency. *Maybe if I really give it some honest effort, I can make some progress on it.* Oddly, it wasn't in the project folder where it should have been. As he looked further, he realized in alarm that most of his project folders contained very few files, and the ones that were there were not important.

Pushing aside his growing sense of panic, he decided to see if he could at least get some paper filing done, a task he had been neglecting for a long time. Even if all he did at the moment was a bit of file reorganization while he thought about his missing computer files, maybe that would be something. He began shuffling through a few files but once again drew back in dismay as he realized that some reorganizing had already been done. The file drawer seemed to contain less than half the number of files it had before. Worse than that, a quick scanning of the remaining files revealed that those he would have tossed out were still there while some very essential files he certainly would have kept were missing.

"No," he groaned. "This can't be happening!" Suddenly he sensed a cold draft. *Was that laughter coming from just beyond the walls?* He shuddered as he remembered the laughter of the demons in his dream.

44

Willing himself to calm down, he tried to think. Then he chided himself, "Get a grip! Something's not right here, but you can fix it!" Desperately he pulled all the files out of the drawers and stacked them on the floor. Then he started to shuffle through and put them into a different order as if that could help. *Surely there is something you can do, there has to be something you can do to fix this!*

"You won't find a solution."

Jumping at the sound of the voice behind him, he turned his head quickly to see The Manager standing just inside his office. Staring at him in speechless dismay, he waited for him to say more.

The Manager quietly returned his stare for a moment before saying, "You have some serious problems here, but if you try to fix it on your own, you will only make matters worse." He paused again before saying solemnly, "We'll talk. Meet me in my office." With that, he turned and left the room.

After placing the files back into the drawer, Bob walked slowly with his head down toward the executive offices. He was not really sure exactly how he would explain himself. From what The Manager had just said, it was obvious that he already knew that paper files were missing. *Does he also know my computer has been accessed and important projects and emails are missing? Does he know I allowed that to happen because I walked away and took a nap? Does he know how little work I've been getting done in the last few weeks, even months?* He tried to imagine what The Manager would say to him. *I'm so disappointed in you, Bob! You are lazy, irresponsible, and incompetent! You're fired!*

He stopped in his tracks for a moment to think. *If he's going to fire me anyway, what's the point of going to talk to him? I might as well just leave right now, and go back to the diner.* He sighed dejectedly. *I hate the diner. I really don't want to go back there. Maybe I can explain to him that I was just really tired, and it's all because people aren't answering my phone calls and emails, and it really isn't my fault that work is so hard. Maybe I can tell him that Charlie is an arrogant jerk.* He shook his head in hopelessness as he realized just how immature and irresponsible all of that would sound. *Well, it has some truth to it.*

He slowly started walking again until he neared the executive offices. He had never approached The Manager's own office without being escorted by an employee with seniority, usually Meredith. Now, as he slowly approached the closed door, he sensed something – an enticing fragrance, an elusive sense of walking through a refreshing mist.

Apprehensively, he walked forward until he was a few steps from the door before stopping again. He was expecting it to open on its own, just as it always did when Meredith brought him here. She never hesitated in front of the door, she simply kept walking and it opened. Now, however, it remained closed. There was no handle, something he had never really noticed before. As he stood still wondering what he should do, he suddenly sensed a faint but compelling voice, "If you move forward, the door will open for you."

Hesitating, Bob glanced around to see if anyone saw him. After all, if he moved forward and the door didn't open, he'd look pretty foolish bumping right into it. The few people in the hall were intent on their own business, so he turned quickly toward the door and took a few deliberate steps. The door did indeed open, allowing him entrance into the outer waiting room before quietly closing behind him.

Bob was quite alone in the room as it had no reception desk, and no one else was waiting to be seen. It was a resplendent waiting area, unlike any he had ever seen. Light from the ceiling cast beams of dancing light so that everything in the room seemed to sparkle. The marble floors were polished and gleaming, and the tables were shimmering with gold etched glass. There was one light that outshone everything, however, and that was a large light directly over the door to The Manager's private office. At the moment, it glowed red. Whenever Meredith had brought him here, they always sat patiently waiting until the light changed to green. Meredith would then stand up and announce with a smile, "The Manager will see us now."

After staring at the red light for a moment, he took a seat and reflected on how he happened to be there. Clearly The Manager already knew important files were missing. It was likely he knew about the missing computer files as well, and even Bob's recent negligence, and maybe even the little nap he had taken. *But if he doesn't, should I just be honest and tell him everything? Bob, you have been such an idiot!* He sighed dismally, recognizing that he had never felt so depressed as he did just now.

The wait seemed long, and he started to fidget restlessly. The light was still red. The Manager would still not see him. Perhaps he should just go back to his desk and somehow try to fix things on his own. The words of The Manager echoed in his mind. *You won't find a solution. If you try to fix it on your own, you will only make matters worse.*

Suddenly something brushed lightly against his sleeve. Startled, he turned to see an angelic being seated right next to him. He had never seen an angel before, and jumped in fright at the sight of him. He had thoughts of getting up and running, but the smiling face gazing back at him was just inches from his own face, leaving him nearly paralyzed by fear.

"You don't want to leave, do you?" the angel asked softly.

Leaning slightly away from him, Bob squeaked out, "Uh, yes, maybe." He was surprised to find he had a voice at all.

"Why do you want to leave? Are things going well for you here?"

Then Bob realized the angel's question was whether he wanted to leave The Company altogether, not whether he would like to get up and flee from the presence of the angel at this particular moment. "No," he replied shakily, "Things are not going, umm, well for me here."

"Are you prepared to talk to The Manager about why things are not going well for you here?" Bob leaned back, trying to put some distance between the angel and himself, but the angel only leaned in closer, staring at Bob intently.

"Umm, I'm, uh, trying to think what I should say to The Manager." His eyes remained inescapably locked with the eyes of the angel.

"Have you considered telling The Manager the truth?"

"The truth?"

"The truth."

Bob was speechless, his mind racing. Memories of feeling burned out with work and an increasingly discouraged and even lazy attitude over the months all came flooding back. *The truth. The truth is I'm tired. The truth is that I have been lazy and negligent. I've had a bad attitude for months. I haven't respected The Manager and I've insulted and even humiliated some of the people I work with. Maybe I should just get up and run, and in fact return to the diner. I'm probably going to be fired now anyway.* Thoughts of returning to the diner made him feel depressed, but timidly he said anyway, "Maybe the truth is that I should, uh, just go back to the diner now."

"Were you happy at the diner?"

"No. I was pretty much miserable all the time at the diner."

"Do you have a future at the diner?"

Some things became clear as Bob pondered the angel's question. If he were to return to the diner, in all likelihood he would be rehired on the spot, because it was difficult for his old boss to find people who were willing to do the menial task of washing dishes, especially since the boss himself was often ill-tempered and at times even hostile. Some people who had taken the job lasted no more than an hour or two before walking out. Bob had prided himself on his ability put up with the man. In a sense they had a "live and let live" approach toward each other. Bob was careful not to let his own laziness and disrespect for his boss and coworkers go so far as to get himself fired, and the boss was careful not to be so cantankerous as to lose an employee who was somewhat willing to put up with his bullying disposition.

Bob imagined himself back at the diner as a dishwasher, with no one who especially cared what he did or didn't do as long as mostly the dishes were washed. He could resume his old careless and irresponsible habits of laziness and disrespect. He might actually feel a sense of freedom from any burden of too much responsibility for a while, but he knew that eventually the truth would catch up with him. There would be no opportunity for meaningful advancement or any sense of fulfillment. He would have enough money to survive, but little hope of ever having more than that. Could that really be called a future? The truth would then be that he had given up and allowed an amazing opportunity to slip away. In that realization he would become all the more hopeless and despairing, and he would begin to yearn for his place back in The Company. He finally answered the angel's question. "No. There is nothing for me at the diner."

"Then what good would it do to go back there?"

"None that I can think of."

The angel leaned in still closer, looming over Bob, who leaned backward until he feared the couch might actually tip over. Again the angel asked the question, this time very slowly and deliberately, one clear word at a time. "Are you ready to tell The Manager the truth?"

If there was even a glimmer of hope to continue working in The Company, would it not have to come from the one who had given him the opportunity in the first place? After a few more moments of serious contemplation in this awkward position, Bob finally said soberly, "Yes. I am ready to tell The Manager the truth."

Smiling, the angel nodded and sat back, finally allowing Bob to sit up straight. There had been a reddish glow reflecting from the angel's face, but suddenly his face took on a greenish hue as he said with a beaming smile, "I believe The Manager will see you now."

Breaking away from the angel's steady gaze, Bob turned to look at the light over The Manager's office door. It had indeed changed to green. The Manager would see him now. He looked back toward the angel only to find that he'd gone and Bob was alone again in the room. Apprehensively and yet with determination, he stood up and slowly approached the door to The Manager's office.

Chapter 7

Unsure what to expect, Bob walked slowly into The Manager's office. He reasoned that in the next few minutes he could very well be gathering up his personal belongings from his office, and then he would be escorted out of the building. He had been feeling so negative about work lately that one might think he would welcome being fired. In his heart he knew it was actually what he feared most.

The Manager was standing behind his desk, but after only a brief moment, he came around the desk and walked straight toward Bob. Although he didn't look angry, Bob backed up slightly, expecting him to say, or possibly even shout, "You're fired!"

There was no shouting. "It's good that you've come to see me, Bob." With an encouraging smile The Manager extended his hand to shake Bob's.

Bob shook The Manager's hand shakily and then stood still for a moment before he realized he needed to be the one to really begin this conversation. Feeling remorseful, he dropped his eyes and stared at his feet. He couldn't think of a thing to say that didn't sound like defensive justification and empty excuses. How could there be any good reason for his indolent behavior?

Are you ready to tell the truth? The words of the angel rang in his ears. Even if he did have a mind now to deny the truth, he knew it wouldn't work; the evidence was all too clear. His once pristinely white uniform was not only gray, it was also now smudged with green grass stains and even had bits of dry grass still clinging to it. Mustering some courage, he raised his eyes and met The Manager's own steady gaze. "Sir, I guess you know there are some very important paper files missing from my office. And emails are missing too, and there are even some essential work projects missing from my computer folders, including the important project you asked about this afternoon that I was – uh, supposed to be working on."

"Yes, Bob, I do know." The Manager nodded and quietly waited for Bob to continue.

Get on with it! You might as well tell him everything and get it over with. Bob blurted out, "Sir, I've been negligent. I've been lazy. I haven't been getting all of my work done for a long time, and today I left my office unattended, and I went outside and I, uh, took a nap. That's why the files are missing, and I know it's my fault. I'm sorry."

"Bob, let's talk about this. You had such a good start when you first began to work for me. What do you suppose led up to your taking a nap?"

There is certainly plenty I could say about the inadequacies of some of my coworkers. It's not exactly like I'm the only one having problems here. Maybe I should at least mention the failures of others. He finally replied "I think it's just that, well, I was having trouble with work. I guess I was frustrated with other people and the work itself just wasn't going very well, and there were problems, and most people seemed intent on their own agendas, and it was like my projects didn't even matter to them. I wasn't getting answers to my phone and email messages, and even when we did manage to communicate, nobody seemed able to make a decision about anything, and there was even arguing about how we should get things done. And then sometimes even when we did manage to accomplish something useful, people wanted to take credit but not give it." *Speaking of not wanting to give credit...* "And well, Sir, Charlie, the mentor that you assigned to work with me... well, we don't really get along very well. He doesn't seem to approve of me somehow. He seems a little, well, bossy or something." He felt like adding that the man was an arrogant, domineering jerk, but he knew that definitely wouldn't be the right thing to do. He shifted his focus and continued, "And then sometimes people outside The Company that a project is intended for don't even appreciate it or receive it well."

He paused as he considered the words of the angel once again. *Are you ready to tell the truth?* Taking a deep breath, he went on, "But Sir, the whole truth is that for a long time I have been feeling overwhelmed and tired and frustrated. And especially in the last few months I've been becoming more and more apathetic and irresponsible. My attitude got worse every day, and I was feeling sorry for myself and even becoming angry because so often things seemed unfair, and I was blaming everyone else not only for their failures, but mine as well. And I started to get bored and my sense of motivation just dried up. I started doing other things like playing internet games when I should have been working. I quit working on some assignments altogether, and I stopped answering some of my emails and phone calls, and, well, I guess that the real reason I went outside to take a nap was because I just plain wanted to give up. I've even had thoughts that maybe I should go back to the diner."

Although Bob felt a sudden sense of relief and even peace that he had finally told The Manager the entire truth, he wondered if at last he would hear the words he dreaded: *You're fired!* His eyes dropped again as he waited for The Manager's reply.

"Bob, look at me." As Bob raised his eyes, he continued, "I'm glad you've decided not to blame others for your failures, because you need to realize I do indeed blame you. You have made some very poor choices indeed. However, you also need to know that I have no interest in firing you."

The Manager was always truthful and very direct at times, and Bob winced inwardly to hear that he blamed him, even though he knew in his heart that blame was rightfully placed. Then he focused on the other thing The Manager had just clearly stated, that he had no interest in firing him. "Uh, you don't?"

"Not in the least. I don't regret having hired you even now in spite of all your failures." The Manager paused for a moment, and then he said, "Bob, I have accepted some of your assignments as incomplete, and as far as you are concerned, that is how they will remain. We can't wait for you. I have told you often that The Door will not stay open forever. Although I have given up on you finishing those specific projects, I will never give up on you. I will never send you back to the diner, Bob."

Bob stared at him with a mixture of relief and confusion. *Why aren't you angry with me? You know that I've been lazy and disrespectful. You know I've been disloyal and dishonest. You know I'm to blame for my indolence. I've failed in my assignments. Why aren't you at least threatening to fire me?*

Suddenly The Manager stepped closer to him and began to brush away the grass that still clung to his shirt. In moments Bob's gray uniform was white again.

"There," The Manager said as he stepped back and surveyed Bob with a smile. "Although you have unquestionably fallen short, you turned around by coming to me and admitting your negligence and failures. Now your uniform reflects the change inside of you. It's just as clean as when you first started with The Company. You see Bob, when you turn around, I always forgive completely. Still, actions which follow poor choices have consequences. Sometimes there are amends you can make for them. Often there is nothing you can do but receive the forgiveness and move on." His expression remained friendly; there was no recrimination.

He let Bob ponder what he had told him for a moment before saying, "Bob, I want you to realize that I certainly appreciate the effort you give when you are trying hard, although that has not been the case most of the time recently. Still, I haven't forgotten the effort you have put in for me and The Company. For example, even this very morning, the completed project you turned in was a job well done. Did I not tell you so?"

Bob nodded contritely and The Manager said, "It gives me no pleasure to have to correct you for foolishness this afternoon." He paused and then continued, "Please don't think that I am indifferent to your problems. I am aware that the work here is often difficult, and coworkers can't always be relied upon, and people outside The Company often are unkind to say the least. All of these things certainly make it challenging for you to get your work done. Not only do these conditions exist, but you have become at least partially aware of the adversarial force at work against The Company, against me, and even against you directly. It is a very dark, evil force which wants nothing more than to see The Company, me, and even you utterly fail."

On hearing this and remembering the demons in his dream, Bob realized the dream had been more than merely a nightmare brought on by his own guilty conscience.

The Manager continued, "Now let's talk about Charlie. I understand in particular the difficulties you have had with him as your mentor. You have received a lot of training since you came on board, and part of Charlie's job was to support and assist you in learning how to put those newly acquired skills into practice. It was wrong of him not to encourage you in the use of your own skills. Not only that, but he was domineering and patronizing, and some of what he had you doing was his own work, and not something you needed to be involved in. When he turned in those projects, he did not acknowledge your contributions to the work. That was unfair. I know that you suspected all along that he was having you do some of his own work and then not even giving you credit for it. Part of the cause for your own discouragement was due specifically to being treated by Charlie, an employee with seniority, in this unfair manner. I am not unsympathetic; I certainly do understand your feelings."

The Manager paused and simply looked with compassion at Bob for a moment before he continued. "However, as I have told you, in your work here you are going to encounter situations with coworkers that will be difficult, challenging and at times completely unfair. I want you to let go of the notion that everything has to seem fair from your perspective for you to behave in an exemplary fashion as my employee. Forgiving someone who you think does not deserve it will perhaps be the most difficult thing you will do in The Company. I want you to trust me. I work on fairness within The Company, and that's my job, not yours. I speak to you about this because of my concern for your own welfare. If you allow yourself to respond to unfair treatment with defensive behaviors and resentment, you cannot move forward. You may even give up again and want to go back to the diner. There you could behave defensively and resentfully all day long if you chose to, and your boss wouldn't even care unless it resulted in lack of productivity and therefore money. I care about you, Bob. I want you to stay focused and keep following me, no matter how difficult that may seem at times, and you can't truly follow me when you are burdened with unforgiveness. As for Charlie, just as you have failed, so has he. That is his own failure, however, and it is between him and me. As of today, he will no longer be mentoring you, but will continue working for me in another location. Bob, will you forgive him? If you will not, how can I forgive you for your own failures? I ask you to forgive him, and let it go."

"Yes, Sir, I forgive him. Well, at least I think I do. I'm trying."

"Forgive him in my name, as my ambassador, realizing that you have faults of your own, and you will find the process of forgiveness attainable. Now, let's move on. So, there are difficulties and opposition to achieving your goals, the completion of your assignments which come from me. Yet in spite of all the obstacles, I place the blame for your failures directly on you. Why do you think that is? Do you suppose that I am actually being unfair?"

Bob contemplated the question before replying sincerely, "No, Sir, you are not unfair. The blame is mine because I should have made better choices. I should have sought your help when there were problems and I didn't know what to do. I should have trusted that you would find a way to help me finish the things you had assigned to me. I should have chosen commitment and loyalty. I should have persevered. I even should have talked to you about Charlie before I became resentful. Instead I allowed myself to get angry and weary and drift. And the longer I drifted, the harder it was to get back on track."

The Manager nodded. "That's right, very good! Now you must keep foremost in your mind that you are forgiven. You and I are going to start over together. The question now is how to get you back to where you were at the beginning." Turning to his desk, The Manager picked up a remote control. "Perhaps we should look at recent events."

Bob had forgotten all about the big screen. He remembered his first day when he and The Manager had looked together at Bob's laziness and poor behaviors in his previous job at the diner. If the Manager knew all about Bob in his old job, he certainly knew all about Bob as an employee of The Company. As if to confirm his fears, the big screen flashed to life with bits and pieces of Bob's recent behaviors at work. There was Bob on screen playing internet games behind his closed office door. The scene changed to show Bob lashing out defensively at a coworker over Bob's own unfinished project. Another scene showed Bob insulting and embarrassing a coworker in a conference room full of employees. And there was Bob, deleting Charlie's last email message to him. The last scene they looked at was Bob asleep on the grassy hillside.

As the screen went blank, The Manager said, "Not exactly you at your best, hmmm? Now let's have a look at the time when you first started with The Company, shall we?"

The big screen flickered to life again, and this time Bob on screen was listening intently to a supervisor who was helping him learn how to do his newly assigned work. The changing scenes showed Bob smiling and offering to help a coworker with a difficult assignment, intently studying the Employee Manual and other training materials, working intently at his computer, and delivering finished assignments on time. A few scenes showed that on many occasions he even stayed and kept working long past the usual 5 p.m. His profound appreciation for the job was evident.

His uniform was pure white and his attitude friendly and relaxed. He looked happy and enthusiastic.

"You were a brand new employee then, and look at your enthusiasm! You didn't know much, but you did know some things. What did you know, Bob?"

Bob reflected before replying, "Well, at first all I really did know was that you hired me in spite of my complete lack of qualifications, and that you were kind and gracious, and you made me your employee."

The Manager smiled and said, "Yes. That about sums it up, doesn't it? You didn't know much, but you knew that you were my employee, hired not on the basis of your own merit, but by my own grace and will." He became more solemn as he asked, "Who are you now, Bob? Because if you don't know who you are, you simply cannot and will not progress from this point."

"Well," Bob said, "I'm still your employee." He faltered, and then added, "I'm just not sure about anything else, except that I guess I need to try harder in my work."

"Yes, you are still my employee. Would I give up on my own child? However, I'm not asking if you are ready to return to being a hard worker. If you merely try harder, the truth is that you will fail again, and you and I will be having this same conversation all over again at some point in the future. Although it's true that I am asking you to give me honest effort, there is so much more to it than just trying harder."

After a pause, The Manager said, "Bob, this is what I am asking you: Are you ready to return to being the person who loved working for The Company, who was thankful not only to have a job here, but also to have me as your Manager? Are you ready to be that person again who was delighted in his new position, who found joy in the smallest details, who listened to my words, and was always ready to learn and willing to submit to my authority even in challenging situations?"

Again, Bob hesitated. Everything The Manager said was true. He had loved The Company, and The Manager, and had been completely thankful for the amazing opportunity he had been given. Still, he hadn't known how difficult the work would become at times, and that some coworkers wouldn't always be so friendly and sincerely helpful as they had seemed at the start. He hadn't known that people on the outside of The Company wouldn't understand, and at times would even be harshly critical of The Company and its employees. He hadn't known that he could become so weary in his labors that he would want to give up.

So what if he did start again, with renewed commitment and zeal, but the problems were still the same as before and the work was still hard and even overwhelming? What if he were to again become discouraged and even angry by the actions and words of coworkers and outsiders? What if the weariness all came back until he felt once again consumed by it? What if he gave up all over again?

"I know what you're thinking, Bob. And the truth is that I cannot tell you that the circumstances which led to your giving up are going to change. They won't. Work will still be difficult, even overwhelming at times, and many coworkers will remain less than cooperative. Some will differ from you in their ideas of what the priorities should be, and how to best accomplish the work. Others will even consider themselves to be superior to you, more important in The Company. Their attitudes will not be helpful to you as far as you accomplishing your work. And there are those who will behave just as you have behaved of late, with self-pity and resentment, with lack of motivation and diligence, and their own failures and attitudes again won't be helpful for you. People outside The Company will continue to not be on your side, and may even show outright hostility toward you."

The Manager suddenly paused and looked down at the floor, obviously deep in contemplation. Bob sensed it was not the time to try to form a response, so he waited quietly. When The Manager looked up again, he asked, "Do you know, Bob, what your biggest problem here has been?"

Bob cleared his throat before hesitantly suggesting, "Laziness?"

"No," The Manager said with a chuckle, "although you have been lazy!" Then he stated soberly, "Your biggest problem is that you have forgotten to consider me your friend. And I am more than a friend to you. You are not merely my employee, you are my beloved employee. Bob, have you not yet recognized that when I gave you a job here, I was adopting you into the family? When did you start to doubt me? When did you stop trusting me? When did you stop listening to me? When did you begin to think of me as your enemy rather than your friend?"

Bob was speechless, so The Manager went on, "I can see you are not sure what answer to give, so I will tell you. When you began to think of work as difficult and burdensome, and that your efforts were not fully appreciated by everyone, that's when you began to stop being lighthearted and enthusiastic. Rather than feeling happy to come in to work each day, you started dreading it. You began to think of me as a taskmaster rather than one who cared about you. You lost trust in me, and worst of all, you began to distance yourself from my presence, all the while hoping I somehow wouldn't notice. As your attitudes continued to decline, you began to fall back into old addictions, things you relied on for comfort and distraction when you worked at the diner. Your obsession with internet gaming is an example of that. When work became difficult here, rather than put your trust in me, you sought comfort in those things again."

Bob knew it was all true, and nodded regretfully.

"So, you see Bob, it's not time for you to just try harder, to run faster. Rather, it's time to slow down and listen. You have developed a very wrong perspective, and that has led to making very wrong choices. It's time for you to not only slow down, but also to turn around and go back." Bob looked puzzled, so The Manager said, "Yes, you need to go back and pick up the perspective you had in the beginning. I am not speaking to condemn you, Bob. My goal is to see you return to being the happy, trusting employee you were at the beginning, yet with a new maturity, a true perspective, and a willingness to persevere. You've already taken the first step. Here you are in my office, confessing your failures, and seeking my help. That first step is always the hardest, but it's also the most important. Now, if you will trust me, I will get you back on track. And if you keep on trusting me, I will walk you to the finish line. Bob, will you trust me?"

Something important occurred to Bob as he considered The Manager's words. He wasn't berating him for his failures, nor threatening to fire him if he didn't get back to work and complete his projects immediately and perfectly. He wasn't saying that if he ever went to sleep on the job again he would be out of The Company. He was actually telling Bob that he wanted him to stay, and that he himself would ensure he would succeed as an employee of The Company. He stood up straighter and returned the Manager's steady gaze. This was all too good to be true, and yet he knew he was hearing only truth. Tears rose up as he replied, "Yes. I will trust you, Sir. Thank you for forgiving me."

"Yes, very good! Bob, I have many things to tell you. We won't get through it all in one day. It's late. We'll start fresh in the morning. Meet me here in my office, first thing. You have returned to me. As you walk out of here I want you to remember what I have told you. I want you to stay focused and stay close." As Bob nodded and started to head toward the door, The Manager added, "Oh, and Bob, one more thing. Wear sturdy shoes tomorrow. You will need them."

Chapter 8

In spite of the cold, Bob could feel sweat beginning to form on his brow. Clinging precariously to the face of the cliff, he looked around for a better grip. There was a somewhat larger hollow in the rock above him, but he wasn't sure he could safely release the grip he already had to reach for it. His toes were jammed into the deepest depressions he could find, but they were feeling less and less secure with every passing minute. As snowflakes swirled about his head in the howling wind, he looked at the frightening drop below, and was bewildered as to how he had managed to climb this high. His knees shook and his fingers began to ache with cold and from gripping the rock while he tried to figure out what to do.

"This can't be right," he muttered. Although his words were snatched away by the fierce wind as soon as he spoke them, he continued to fume out loud anyway. "Where'd The Manager go? How'd I lose the path?"

He thought about how the day had started out. He had arrived for morning coffee chat with The Manager feeling hopeful, thankful, and eager to get started again. Having early morning coffee chats with The Manager had been part of his routine when he had first begun his new position in The Company. He had looked forward to them eagerly, knowing he would be learning new things and that he would be encouraged just by spending time with him. However, it was one of the first things Bob had let go of when his attitudes began to slide.

This time was different from the coffee chats of the past, however. They had not been talking for long before The Manager stood up and said, "Bob, let's go for a walk." Then he had handed him a water bottle, and they had left the building together. It had been a beautiful morning with plenty of sunshine and not a hint of the storm they would soon be engulfed in.

At first they had walked side by side, talking as they hiked up the gentle slope. Gradually the gentle slope had turned into a steep and winding rocky hill, and bit by bit The Manager had gotten ahead of him. Bob had kept his eyes on him and followed, amazed at his unflagging strength. At times The Manager had even run uphill, leaving Bob to try to catch up as he wondered just how unlimited The Manager's strength actually was. Bob had also wondered just what he had in mind and where the path would take them. Occasionally he had stopped to take a drink of cool water from the bottle, but when he did The Manager had just seemed to get even further ahead, so Bob had found himself running uphill as well at times just to keep him in view. Eventually, however, he had lost sight of him completely and now found himself in this dire predicament.

"You idiot!" he scolded himself. "Why didn't you just keep up?" He looked again at the small grip above his head, and then back to the depths below. His strength was beginning to fade, and he wondered just how long he had been stuck like this. He knew he had to make a decision of some sort, even if it was to give up and try to get back down. He looked below and tried to see the same toe and hand holds he had used to get this far. *I'm so tired. But I don't want to give up, I really don't. Besides, if I try to get back down I might fall...* With a sudden start, he realized in his indecisiveness he had closed his eyes for more than a moment. Drowsiness now threatened to overcome him. *Bob, you dope, you can't stay here like this, make a decision before you fall asleep!*

His eerie sense of utter isolation was suddenly broken as a sinister voice spoke contemptuously out of the swirling snow. "Loser! You know you're too weak for this. Once again you've done nothing more than prove you can't be relied on to do anything right. It's freezing cold and The Manager has left you all alone. This is grueling; who do you think you are, trying to run uphill anyway, and now look at you! You're much too tired to go on, why don't you just give up? You're going to die trying to get off this stupid cliff anyway!" Malicious laughter followed the dire predictions, and then the howling wind was once again all that Bob could hear.

That evil thing is right, I'm going to fall and I'm going to die, and no one will even care, that is if they ever do find me. Shaking off the morbid thoughts, Bob tried to focus instead on something The Manager had said while they were walking earlier that morning. *"Bob, I am never really as far away* as you might think. When the going gets tough, and it will get tough, the most important thing you can do is remember that I am always there for you. Simply do not give up. Don't worry, don't panic, and don't give up."

Maybe this would be a good time to talk to The Manager as if he were present. Looking up, he tried to see through the gray skies and blizzard to the top of the cliff. He thought he could make out a blurry figure just a couple of feet above him, or was it just some trickery of the wind and snow? Taking a gulp of air and tightening his grip on the rock, he hesitantly managed to squeak out, "Sir? Mr. Manager? Help me!"

Suddenly the shadowy figure above him became more distinct, and a hand reached down to him. "Up here, Bob! You're almost at the top, so let go of the rock and grab my hand, I will help you!" Quickly Bob reached out to grab the hand The Manager was extending to him. The Manager's grip was strong and steady, and the next thing he knew, Bob was sitting next to him on the cliff top, gulping air while he tried to stop shaking.

The Manager was smiling at Bob as if he had just finished a marathon. "Good job, you made it!"

Bob took a few more deep breaths before he replied, "Thank you for the hand up!" He felt overwhelmed as he thought about what had just happened. Only moments before, he had been in sheer terror and near despair. He glanced at The Manager with a mixture of thankfulness and awe, but also a sense of disquiet. Being rescued was so unexpected, and yet, should I not have known? He said he would never be as far away as I might think. Why was I even beginning to panic?

After letting Bob catch his breath, The Manager stood up. "Let's move on, shall we?" With that he turned and started down the path, leaving Bob to get up and follow. Shortly they were walking down a rocky hillside on a path that took them away from the cliff and the freezing storm. Bob could see a green meadow below, with wildflowers dotting the wavy grass, and a stream meandering through it. Best of all, the sun was once again shining brightly.

Soon however, it began to get warmer, and then even hot. Sweat began to form on his brow. His feet were tired, and he was thirsty. He regretted that he'd had to abandon his water bottle when the cliff had become too steep to hold it any longer. But The Manager was getting ahead of him again, so he put aside all thoughts of discomfort and hastened to keep him in sight.

At last they were in the meadow, and had almost reached the rippling stream. The Manager suddenly slowed his pace and allowed Bob to catch up. "Come on, it's time for a break!" Turning abruptly, he then left the path and headed directly toward the stream, beckoning for Bob to follow. When they reached it, he sat down and began to remove his shoes and socks. Bob looked at him quizzically, but he motioned for Bob to do the same, and shortly they were both sitting on rocks and bathing their feet in the cool, soothing stream under the cool shade of a large tree.

Handing Bob a water bottle and a granola bar, The Manager looked perceptively at him and then said, "You know you have yet to smile."

"Sir, I'm very thankful – you rescued me! I really think I might have fallen back there. But Sir, I'd like to apologize. I didn't keep up, and I got behind and then lost, and I ended up stuck on that cliff."

"Yes, you did get a little behind. But Bob, let me ask you a question. Do you assume that because the trail had become so difficult, you had gotten onto the wrong path?"

Bob thought for a moment. Perhaps he was misunderstanding something, but that was exactly what he had been thinking. "Well, yes, it seemed like you weren't around, and I know it was my fault and I should have tried harder to keep up with you, and then I was on that cliff and there was all that snow, and wind, and it was so cold, and the cliff was really steep, almost vertical even, and then there was this evil voice coming out of the storm telling me I was a loser and I was going to die, and I should just give up!" Bob sighed dejectedly. "It just didn't seem like the right path at all."

"Yes, the way became extremely difficult and challenging, and I seemed far away, and the evil voice was trying to discourage you from continuing. But then what happened?"

"Well, I remembered that just this morning you told me that you would never be as far away as I might think. And so I thought I should talk to you and ask for help, and I hoped you would hear me."

"Yes, and of course I did hear you because I didn't leave you alone, just as I told you. Then I helped you because you needed my help. Bob, it is important to keep your eyes focused on me. If you follow me, you won't get lost. But you also need to know that I am proud of you. You didn't give up even at the trail's toughest point!"

Bob felt a little confused. "You're proud of me? So, you mean it was the right path all along, and I wasn't lost at all?"

"Bob, if you think the existence of trouble in your path is evidence that the path is not of my choosing, then you will refuse to go forward whenever you encounter it. Although it's true that sometimes difficulties encountered can be evidence of a wrong path, that's certainly not always the case. The truth is that in your work for me you will always have difficulties. At times your work may seem easy and even fun, and during those times you will feel enthusiastic about doing the work. But there will also be times when doing the work feels more like when you were clinging to that cliff. You were engulfed in a storm, it was grueling, and it was all you could do to just hold on! You became tired and scared and started to doubt you were doing the right thing. You wanted to give up and go back, but you made a choice to call on me instead. You took hold of my hand and with my help you overcame that cliff and then you moved forward, still following me. Trust me in this. For you to succeed in The Company there will be many times you will have to persevere through difficulties, and not just try to find an easy way around them.

"Think of it as a race. Your goal in a race is to arrive at the finish line first, ahead of your adversary. But it's not enough to merely start well, or go faster, or try harder for a time. You must be determined to go the distance. You have to have the mind set to finish. You can't even toy with the notion of dropping out. If you do, when you encounter obstacles in your race, dropping out will become all you are able to think about. Just as obstacles are part of a race, obstacles in your everyday work are just part of the nature of work itself. If you are mentally prepared ahead of time, knowing they will be there, yet also knowing that I am your greatest ally and friend, your mind will be set on finishing the race, not on dropping out because the difficulty is great. Bob, I will always be there for you. I don't even want you to think about dropping out, do you understand?"

Bob nodded, and then The Manager added, "And yes, I'm proud of you. You felt lost, and you were also drained of strength. You felt like giving up, but you demonstrated courage by not doing so. You listened to what I had said to you earlier, and you remembered it when the way became too tough for you to manage. And then you showed trust in me by calling out to me for help and taking the hand I extended to you."

Bob thought for a while, then said, "So, you're saying that sometimes if I have trouble it's because I'm not going in the direction you want me to go, but other times it doesn't mean that at all, and I have to find a way through the trouble and not take the easy way around it?"

"Yes, I am saying that."

Bob was perplexed. "But then, how will I know the difference? If I have trouble in my work how will I know whether to change what I'm doing or keep moving forward?"

The Manager smiled. "It might seem like a simple formula for all situations would be the right thing, but the truth is that if you have a formula, then you don't need to rely on me. I value your reliance on me, highly in fact, and not so much your ability to manage everything on your own. I am not looking for you to succeed by applying the same formula to each individual situation. I am also not asking you to do everything in your own strength. You are learning the most important thing you can learn, and that is to rely on and trust me. It's something I want you to remember always."

Bob remembered having questions for his old boss at the diner, and how he had been snapped at and berated for not figuring it all out on his own. *Isn't self-reliance one of the most important traits for any employee to have, and isn't always bothering The Manager with work related issues a wrong thing to do?*

Seeing his still questioning stare, The Manager asked, "Bob, how well were you managing that cliff on your own?"

"Not well at all, I might have fallen without your help!"

"And did I in any way scold you for needing my help and calling out to me?"

"No, you just helped me!"

"Yes. No reproach. I just helped you. Bob, you can believe in yourself, and in your own efforts, or you can believe in me. It's actually a difficult and sometimes confusing choice, but one that all my employees have to make, even on a daily basis."

Bob sat in quiet contemplation. He finally allowed a smile to appear as he said, "Thank you, Sir. I'm very glad you are proud of me. That means more to me than maybe anything. I'll remember what you've said, and I will try to remember to seek your help always, especially when I feel tired and confused and don't know which way to turn." He felt a certain sense of peace as they continued to sit quietly enjoying the serenity of the stream and shade under the trees.

Chapter 9

The very next morning, The Manager wasted no time in helping Bob to get going in the right direction again. They had been enjoying coffee and talking everything over for a while when The Manager said, "There is something very important you have been missing out on even though it has been available to you from your first day here. A great deal of your trouble has been due not only to thinking that you had to do the work in your own strength, but also thinking that you could do the work in your own strength. Now you know both, that you don't and that you can't. I've assigned Meredith to help you in the matter of receiving strength from me beyond your natural limitations. She actually did try to help you on your first day with this unique bestowing, but you allowed fear and ignorance to hinder your openness to receiving it."

The Manager then pressed the green light button allowing Meredith to enter the office. After greeting her and giving her a brief explanation of her assignment, The Manager dismissed the two of them and they left his office together.

Bob was surprised that she led him straight to the break room. Looking at her doubtfully, he said, "A snack now? Meredith, is this really necessary?" The usual smell of donuts and coffee wafted through the air. Meredith ignored them and headed straight for the vending machine in the back of the room. Bob grabbed a donut before joining her hesitantly. He wasn't too sure anything in that machine right now could help his present circumstances.

She turned to see him starting to take a bite from the donut. "Put that down, Buster!"

His eyes widened in surprise at her fervor. Then it dawned on him that the thing she had tried to help him with on his first day was to be open to receiving a specific anointing oil that was available from the vending machine. He thought about what The Manager had just said, that he had allowed his fears and ignorance to hinder his willingness to receive it. Now he knew it was time to trust The Manager again, and allow Meredith to open a bottle and pour it on his head. This had always seemed like a strange thing to Bob, and as he thought about it now, he realized it actually was a very strange thing indeed. *In what other company would you ever find such a thing?* He dutifully put the donut down on a nearby table.

Meredith stood facing him and said solemnly, "Bob, this I do in the name of The Manager. I anoint you with the oil of His Presence."

Bob couldn't help but say, "Please don't use too much." He was remembering the matted down oily hair of employees who had recently received the anointing. He was also remembering how some had acted after receiving the oil. There was often laughter for no apparent reason, and nonstop talking about The Manager and how wonderful he was. There was even talk about things Bob had not been able to understand how they knew, like what retirement would be like, and things pertaining to the worldwide promotion of The Company. He didn't know much about those things, and he surely didn't want to appear like a laughing fool!

"I pour, that's all. It's not up to me how much comes out. And, it's not for you to worry about either. Do you trust the Manager or don't you?"

Bob nodded slowly. "Yes, I do trust the Manager. And I guess I have to trust you now, too, don't I?"

Suddenly they both felt a cold draft, as if a window had been opened to a cold and stormy outside. They turned to see two black-cloaked figures gliding swiftly toward them and the vending machine.

Acting just as quickly, Meredith took a few purposeful steps directly toward them. "You have no part in this! Be gone in the name of the Manager!" Her words were tough and unyielding.

Although the two stopped and backed up slightly, they looked at Bob questioningly, as if to see if he might be willing to let them stay. One of them said almost pleadingly, "Bob, what are you doing here? You've been doing fine all along, just fine, all on your own! You don't need anything from the vending machine! Grab a cup of coffee and a donut, and come with us, and we'll go someplace to talk about this!"

Bob sensed their sly and devious plan, and also knew it was up to him not to yield to it. "Get out of here! I agree with Meredith, we both tell you to leave in the name of The Manager!"

As quickly as he said that, the two turned and glided away, the cold air retreating with them.

Meredith turned back to Bob almost as if the interruption hadn't happened. "Yes, it will most certainly help if you trust me too! You need this. You aren't strong enough to do the work for the Manager without it. You need joy and strength and power and peace. You also need confidence. All of these things come from the presence of The Manager alone!" She opened the bottle, stretched her arm over his head and poured out the contents.

At first Bob felt only the oil itself, but then a warm sensation began to grow until it seemed to envelop his entire being. His heart felt light, and he wondered how he ever could have been so tired and stressed in the first place. Things suddenly seemed obvious. He remembered now how he had come to work at The Company with no power to do anything. How had he managed to forget that he didn't have a single shred of ability to do anything whatsoever within The Company apart from The Manager? Relief flooded him, along with a peaceful sense of knowing that now all would be okay.

Meredith was watching him closely, studying his face. He couldn't help smiling at her. He had always been fond of her, as though she were his very own grandmother. That affection now rose up strongly. He laughed slightly, and then, to his own surprise, he hugged her. "Thank you, Meredith! You're wonderful!" He laughed again, his sense of delight growing.

She relaxed from her staunch attitude and smiled back at him in approval that the oil had taken its proper effect. She then said, "Now you have the joy of The Manager. Now you have the strength of The Manager. Now you know it's not about you doing the work in your own limited ability. Therefore, now you can do the work that needs doing!"

Bob wasn't inclined to disagree in the least. At last, everything made sense.

Later that afternoon, Bob and The Manager were having a discussion in Bob's office when The Manager said, "Bob, you've learned some very important lessons the last few days. Tell me what they are."

Bob nodded. "Well, I've learned that you are my friend. That's the most important thing. And I've learned that you always care, and you want to help me be successful. And that I should not be afraid to bring my problems to you. And that you are always there for me. And I shouldn't give up when the path becomes difficult." Bob felt like he could go on and on, but The Manager was chuckling, and Bob sensed that was enough for now.

"Good, very good!" The Manager looked thoughtful and then said, "There is another matter which we need to address, something that has contributed significantly to the difficulties you have had lately, and that is your avoidance of employee meetings. Bob, can you tell me what happens when you stop gathering together with your coworkers?"

"Well, things don't get better, that's for sure!"

"You have a tendency to become isolated, do you not?"

Bob nodded in agreement as he thought about all the meetings he had skipped out on lately using any excuse he could find to cover his absence. He knew his avoidance of the meetings was based not only on fears of what his coworkers might think of him if they knew how much he was struggling with work issues, but also fears that some of them might even try to help him if they did know. Of late he had definitely not been open to receiving help. Another reason he had been avoiding the meetings was he didn't want to risk being around some of the very coworkers he was feeling the most resentful toward.

He remembered a time when he had looked forward to attending the meetings with eagerness. Most of his coworkers were friendly, helpful and encouraging, even compassionate. He quickly learned to rely on them for help and advice in any situation. Sometimes the purpose of a meeting was to study and help each other gain insight from The Employee Manual. Often meetings were held by employees who were working together on the same project. Sometimes the purpose of a meeting was more a social gathering, a way of getting to know each other better while having a refreshing break from work. Whatever the purpose of the meetings, he had left them feeling refreshed and encouraged, even strengthened.

The work he accomplished was then even more prolific and on target. Avoiding the meetings had only resulted in a greater lack of productivity on his part as well as fostering his sense of weary discouragement.

"Bob, I told you when you first started that much of what you will learn and much of my help you will receive in your employment will come through others, your coworkers, your adopted family if you will. You can't be built up into the family of The Company if you don't spend time with your brothers and sisters. So, starting today, you will begin attending the meetings and catch up on some of the fellowship you've missed. There happens to be a special sort of meeting going on right now down in Lower B, and I would like for you to join with them in what they are doing. It's a special opportunity for you to be useful and make a difference."

As Bob walked to Lower B, he wondered just what the meeting might be all about. He knew the entire lower level had been closed for renovations for some time. There hadn't been any announcement indicating it was open and ready for use, so he was puzzled as to how there could be a meeting taking place there. But when he arrived in the room The Manager had indicated, he realized exactly what was going on. Many employees he recognized were there, hard at physical labor, helping the construction crew to finish the renovations.

One of them stopped hammering and called out, "Hey, Bob, welcome! We need all the hands we can get!"

Bob soon found himself holding drywall in place and even hammering nails. Although it felt humbling to be doing physical labor, something not listed in his job description, he realized the importance of getting the renovations finished so the rooms could be used again. The lack of available conference rooms was often a source of complaining and even arguing among the employees. He could see now that working to help alleviate the problem was much more effective than complaining and arguing. He also enjoyed simply being active, and the chatter that went on while everyone worked was refreshing.

At the end of the day Bob was tired physically, but otherwise he felt renewed and somehow very satisfied. As he headed back toward the offices with a few of the others who had been helping, it occurred that they were the few coworkers who knew how he had spent his day. There had been a few simple words of thanks for helping them out, but beyond that he knew the people he worked with weren't even aware that he had spent the day in hard labor to accomplish something useful for all of them. There would be no special recognition, no one saluting him and saying thanks, great job! Even as those thoughts registered, he remembered that The Manager knew how he had spent his day. The Manager knew that he had been obedient to this special assignment and that he had worked diligently for the sake of others. Bob had no sense of disappointment; rather he had a deep sense of contentment. *Knowing that he is pleased, that is enough for me.*

Chapter 10

A few weeks later, Bob stood chatting casually with Amy in a conference room that was rapidly filling with employees. They had gathered in response to an email from Management which stated that a new website for The Company was being planned. Anyone who would like a chance to be on the team being formed to create and maintain the website should report to the conference room for evaluation and skill assessment.

Until recently, Bob would have just ignored the email. However, as part of the ongoing training and education The Manager had encouraged him to sign up for, Bob was currently taking classes to learn how to create a website. He found that he not only enjoyed learning the skill, but actually had some aptitude for it. He was getting fairly high scores as a result of his enthusiasm.

The Manager had also told him to be alert and on the lookout for new and challenging opportunities. This would certainly be both new and challenging. *But me? Can I really do this? Am I ready for such a thing? Should I even be in this room at all?* As he glanced apprehensively around the room, he couldn't help but think that the true computer experts in the room had to be regarding him with at least a little contempt. He noticed they had perhaps subconsciously grouped together on one side of the room like members of an elite club.

When laughter broke out among them, Bob wondered if possibly they were laughing at his own audacity in showing up for this. The thought made him cringe inwardly. *I could pretend I just remembered something important to do back at my desk and get out of here.* But something else The Manager had said occurred to him. *To be truly effective, sometimes you have to be brave and take risks you might more naturally choose to avoid.* Lifting his chin a bit, he stood still and tried to tune in to Amy's casual chatter.

Amy's presence in the room reassured him somewhat. He knew that although she tinkered with some blogging and computer art on the side, she wasn't anywhere close to having the capability of building a website from scratch. "I don't know, Amy, what do you think?" Bob spoke quietly so others in the room wouldn't hear. "I mean, look at all the computer geeks in the room! Think we stand a chance?"

Amy sighed pessimistically as she looked around the room. "Probably not. Why do you suppose the email didn't spell out the prerequisites for a spot on the team? Usually that sort of thing is all spelled out, you know."

Bob had also been wondering about the email. Possibly an admin had forgotten to include prerequisites when typing up the information. If so, perhaps the meeting would begin with a simple announcement letting everyone know of the omission and allowing those not qualified to get back to work. Or, maybe prerequisites were somewhat relaxed because the intent was to have a team quickly build a simple site from a template, something almost anyone could do. *Click to add slideshow. Click to add paragraphs.* But even if quick and easy were the intention, it still seemed likely that those with superior skills and training would be chosen over those with lesser qualifications for something as important as The Company Website. Deciding not to voice his speculations, he answered Amy's question with, "I don't know. Maybe we ought to just head back to our offices. I mean, we do have important work waiting for us, right? This could all be just a big waste of time."

"Yeah, you're probably right," Amy agreed, yet neither moved toward the door.

Their opportunity to quietly back out vanished as The Manager suddenly entered the room and closed the door. Along with the other candidates, Bob and Amy found seats while The Manager greeted those present with, "Thank you all for showing an interest in being on The Company Website Team. I know you have other important things to be doing, so please be assured that I appreciate your commitment of time to these proceedings." There was no announcement to indicate prerequisites had been neglected. An encouraging smile from The Manager assured Bob that he was indeed welcome in the room, so he relaxed and focused on The Manager's speech.

"The focus of today's testing will primarily be skill assessment in the area of website construction. As you can see, the computers have already been set up for this purpose. Although you will be creating an actual website, it is for evaluation purposes only, and the resulting websites will not be prolonged beyond the scope of this class. Now if you would, please turn your attention to the printed set of instructions we've placed with each computer. It gives you content to display, but does not include the proper syntax on how to do that. A folder has been created on our Company intranet which contains the content to be included on your site, such as images, and some Company information, both basic and more advanced, along with supplementary text for filling empty space with additional content of general interest. Remember, the purpose of this evaluation is primarily to see how much you already know. Take some time and care because we have allowed the entire day for this portion of the evaluations. If you happen to finish your website before the day is over, you may further improve your basic site with creative enhancements at your own discretion.

"Our evaluation process does not end at the finish of this day – the testing will continue tomorrow and the following day with more advanced exams to be set up in another conference room. If you finish the construction of your website to my satisfaction today, you will have the opportunity to move on to the next part of the exam tomorrow. The testing will last for three days. At the conclusion, I will analyze your websites, and we will all know who will be approved for possible placement on the team. Questions?"

After a few questions had been asked and answered, the exam began and Bob began setting up the computer files he would need to build his site according to the instructions outlined in the paper packet. Style sheets were not part of what was already provided so he would have to write his own. He wished he'd had time to brush up on the proper syntax. *Brackets have to set apart each declaration. Let's see, is that right? No. Brackets set apart the declarations from the – uh, selector. Semi-colon has to separate each declaration within the brackets. Ummm, is that right? Let's see, should I use tables – or 'div' for organizing the content? 'Div,' I think. Whew, this is going to be a long day!*

Bob continued to move the mouse and peck at the keyboard, using what he could remember along with trial and error to see what worked, until a break was called. Sitting back, he quickly reviewed his site so far. *Not bad! I guess I remembered more than I thought I would.*

The rest of the day went by quickly, including lunch and a few short breaks, and at last The Manager called an end to the day's testing. After reviewing each website briefly and making some notes, he stood at the head of the room and announced who the successful finishers of that day's testing were. Bob was both surprised and pleased to find himself among them. "Those who are in this group will have the opportunity to move on to subsequent testing tomorrow," The Manager said. *Why does he keep saying 'opportunity to move on,' as though there would be any other choice?* Bob didn't have to wonder long.

"Now I have a question just for those of you who are qualified to move ahead," The Manager said. "Rather than moving on to the more advanced tests, are there any of you who would be willing to stay back in this same conference room tomorrow to help the candidates who did not succeed today? With some help, they could possibly succeed well enough to finish up their websites and move ahead as well."

All eyes were on The Manager. Bob was speechless along with the other successful finishers. *What? Stay back and possibly lose too much time to complete the rest of the evaluations? And as a result miss out on the exciting opportunity to be on the website team? All for the sake of helping someone else?* He was sure the others were having dubious thoughts as well. No hands were raised as a gesture to volunteer. The silence seemed unending.

At last The Manager said, "Very well! I shall see you all in Room 214 tomorrow, and the rest of you may return to this room to finish your websites to the best of your ability, without help from anyone."

Shifting uncomfortably in his seat, Bob glanced around as people began to pick up belongings and make their exit. He noticed with some sadness that Amy was not in the group of those who had successfully completed the day's evaluation. Her disappointment was apparent as she gave him a half-hearted smile and left the room.

Wanting to appear occupied, Bob remained seated and shuffled through some papers. The Manager exchanged small talk with a few of the employees as they exited until finally he and Bob were left alone in the room.

"Something on your mind, Bob? You did very well on your website, you know. I'm proud of you and your renewed effort."

"Thank you, Sir. I really enjoy website construction. It seems more like fun than work."

The Manager nodded. "It's good to find out what you enjoy and are good at. Work doesn't always have to be tedious. You have unique aptitudes; not everyone can do what you can do. I'm glad you've decided not to run from your destiny. So, what are you looking troubled about?"

"Well – the ones who didn't finish. Do you think they will finish well enough to move on with us after tomorrow?"

"They will continue to struggle without help. I don't think it likely they'll catch up."

"And you would really like someone to stay back and help them?"

"Yes, I would really like that. Are you interested in helping the others, Bob?"

"Well, it seems kind of a bummer that some of them have talents but they can't be on the team just because they lack the technical skill. You know, like Amy. She's definitely not a computer geek, but she has some artistic and graphic design skills that might actually be an asset to the team."

"That's a very good assessment, Bob. Would you like to volunteer to help Amy and the others succeed?"

Bob hesitated as he pondered the situation. It occurred to him that the furthest thing from his mind before he had left the building to take a nap was how he might please The Manager. Now he knew his desire to please him was not only restored, it was greater than it ever had been. It was even greater than his desire right now to be on the website team. Another thought occurred to him, and that was that he actually did want to help the others succeed, especially friends like Amy. Still, the choice wasn't easy, and even felt painful. What he was about to say could very well keep him off the team. With a sense of commitment he finally spoke quietly, "Yes, I would like to help the others. I will come back here in the morning if that's what you want."

The Manager beamed. "Son, you are making an excellent choice. I'll see you back here in the morning!"

The next morning, Bob popped into Amy's office on his way back to the conference room. She was at her desk, but leaning toward the window and staring outside. "What's up, Amy? Are you ready to get back to the website evaluations?"

"Oh, hi, Bob. Actually, I think I'm having second thoughts. I just don't see much reason for me to continue the testing – I really haven't learned website construction enough to do any better today than I did yesterday, so I'm not sure there's any point in going back." She shrugged indifferently, and then added, "Besides, I have a lot to do. I'm just having a bit of trouble getting started on my work this morning, that's all."

"I know you're probably feeling tired and discouraged, but please join us back in the conference room again today. I'm staying back in the same room with you all, and maybe I can help you enough to make a difference on your websites."

Amy stared at him incredulously. "You're staying back? To help us?"

Bob nodded. "Yep. The Manager would really like for someone to stay and help the ones who didn't finish yesterday, and really, why are we here if not to please The Manager?"

"Well, sure, but if you don't keep up with the others, you'll probably lose your chance to be on the team!"

"Yeah, I know that's likely to happen, but I've been doing a lot of thinking, and it seems to me that pleasing The Manager has to come before my own personal ambitions, and as long as I remember that, then somehow everything will work out okay. I know this will likely cost me a spot on the team, and I have to admit that I feel disappointed about that, but honestly, this is the only choice I feel good making right now."

Amy stared at Bob with a mixture of perplexity and admiration. "Gosh, Bob, I get what you're saying, but I'm just not sure I could make that choice!"

Bob shrugged as if it were no big deal. "So, come on, let's see what we can make of that website of yours today!" Amy assented somewhat reluctantly, and they went to the conference room to join the group.

For that day and the next, Bob worked with the group in a positive and steady fashion. He did his best to be clear in his instructions as well as patient. As he did so, he discovered that he not only enjoyed teaching others how to design and construct a site, but was gaining more understanding of it himself as he explained it to them.

On the morning following the three full days of testing, all of the participants were once again seated in the original conference room waiting for The Manager to reveal the final results. Although seats had not been assigned, the contestants had perhaps subconsciously grouped themselves according to placement in the exams – those who had moved on successfully the first day were together on one side of the room while Bob and those he had stayed back to help were on the other. Bob couldn't help but notice that a few of those across the room looked pretty self-satisfied. They sat back casually in their chairs, arms crossed over their chests, half-smiles on their faces.

"I hate smug!" With that abrupt statement, The Manager had the full attention of everyone in the room. Looking astutely at everyone he added, "Today you are all in for some surprises!"

Why would everyone be surprised? Bob shifted in his chair and glanced around the room uncertainly, his gaze resting again on those across the room. *Smug. Are they who The Manager is referring to?* He looked back at The Manager and focused on what he was saying.

"As you all know, some of the contestants did quite well from the first day, and moved on to the subsequent exams. We'll talk about them first. Some of the people from that group excelled, and are to be congratulated. They gave it their best effort all the way to the finish, with the end result of some remarkable websites. I am impressed with their overall results. On the other hand, there are also a few in that group who did not finish as successfully as they might have. I would like for those individuals to consider that overconfidence and a presumptive attitude can cause a lack of wholehearted effort. In other words, when you are already sure you will win, you stop racing strongly all the way to the finish. We will leave it at that for now and talk about the other group."

The Manager turned toward the group seated with Bob and continued, "This group, with the exception of one individual, did not do as well from the first day, and so did not have the opportunity to move on with the first group. However, with some help, they have in the end achieved perhaps far more than they ever thought they could. I would like to congratulate and thank them for returning to this room and investing sincere effort in spite of the setback of the first day."

"Now the question on everyone's mind, of course, is: 'Who won? Who will be awarded the few positions on The Company website team?' Well, as I said, you are all in for some surprises. I remind you all that from the beginning, I never said The Company website would be built by that one single individual possessing the greatest skill and expertise in website development. I have always said we would be putting together a team to do the work. One of the most important traits of any good team member is to be concerned for the rest of the team. That's what makes a team a team – a willingness to do what it takes to help the whole team succeed." The Manager paused as he let his words soak in. Everyone sat up straighter and stared at him.

"I gave those of you who successfully passed the testing on that first day a very special opportunity, but only one was willing to even consider it. The opportunity was to stay back and help the others become successful as well. Of course, the assumed risk of that opportunity was the possibility of losing the chance to be on the team at all. The one individual who was willing to take that risk is the one I have decided not only to grant a position on the team, but to appoint as our new website team leader. Please join me in welcoming Bob to his new assignment as leader of The Company Website Team!" The Manager smiled at Bob encouragingly and said, "Bob, please stand up."

This was quite unexpected, and it took Bob a moment to stand shakily to his feet. He kept his eyes on The Manager, but he could feel the stares of everyone in the room. At first the room was quiet as the shock of The Manager's announcement sank in. Then a ripple of enthusiastic applause sprang from among those Bob had stayed behind to help. It took most of those seated on the other side of the room a few moments to join in with a smattering of polite clapping.

The Manager continued speaking. "Many of you probably know that Bob is new to the skill of developing a website, and therefore not the most proficient at it. There are, in fact, several people in this room whose technical skills far exceed his own. However, to be a good team leader of any given project, you don't necessarily have to possess the greatest knowledge nor the highest skill level pertaining to that project. Pure selfish ambition may help a person become more qualified in some areas of expertise, but that isn't what makes an individual a good team member, and it can never be a desirable quality in a team leader. The team leader is that individual who is visionary, not for himself alone, but who recognizes the overall purpose of both the team and its project, and who can organize and direct the team to achieve that purpose. He is one who considers how to best utilize the skills and talents of each team member to the advancement of the goals of the team.

"Most of you pretty much assumed that the only thing that mattered was proving your skill and knowledge to be superior. Bob proved to me he could successfully lead this team when he took a step back from the competition and considered first what was important to me, and then how he might help the others as well.

"Bob, you can sit down now." He nodded at Bob who thankfully sat down. "I have made clear my choice of Bob as the team leader. If any of you are inclined to disagree, I ask you to trust me as your Manager and respect him in his new position. As the team leader, he will need the help and support of many of you here in this room."

He paused and surveyed the group quietly for a moment, then said, "Bob's first assignment in his new role will be to fill out the team roster. With my counsel, Bob will choose the prospective team members from among all of you. If you are selected, you will receive an invitation from Bob to attend the first official team meeting. Now if there are no questions, you are all dismissed. Again, I thank you for your time."

Chapter 11

"Thank you everyone for coming to this meeting. As you all know, I have invited you here…" A knock on the door of the small conference room interrupted Bob's attempt to get the website team's preliminary meeting started. Thinking it was someone arriving a bit late, he stood up from the table and opened the door. The woman standing there was well known to all in The Company. Surprised, it took Bob a moment before he managed to greet her with, "Oh, uh, hi Priscilla!"

With a somewhat haughty look Priscilla said, "The Manager sent me. Mind if I join you?" Without waiting for a response, she entered the room and took a moment to coolly survey the attendees. Then she walked briskly toward an empty seat, her high heels clicking sharply on the tile floor. Placing a notebook on the table, she adjusted one of her sparkly earrings and brushed an invisible bit of fuzz from her silk blouse. Apparently satisfied that her appearance was flawless, she sat down and folded her hands on the notebook in front of her. The patronizing half-smile she gave to Bob indicated she was ready for him to begin the meeting.

Bob grimaced slightly. *As if this were not already nerve-wracking enough…* He sat back down and stared at the agenda he'd come up with.

The Manager and he had talked in preparation for this first meeting, and The Manager had explained to him some of the priorities and objectives of the website. They had also discussed the potential team members and the role each individual might fill on the team. With the insights he had gained from listening to The Manager, Bob had selected prospective team members and sent emails to them inviting them to attend this first meeting.

However, some who were invited had replied with excuses, saying for one reason or another they had to decline the invitation. Bob knew that for some at least, the real reason they no longer wanted to be on the team was that they weren't happy with The Manager's choice of himself as the team leader. Bob was actually glad that some had chosen not to attend because it would simply make it easier to fill out the roster. He was confident now that most anyone still wanting to be on the team would have a position.

Inexplicably, a few who weren't happy had for some reason shown up anyway, and their displeasure was evident on their faces. One in particular Bob felt was surely going to be a problem. When Jed had entered the room, he had given Bob a look that bordered on hostility before silently taking a seat and crossing his arms defiantly across his chest. Having to proceed with him at the table was disconcerting to say the least.

And now Priscilla was here. Glancing around at those present, Bob realized he was not the only one feeling intimidated by her presence. Most didn't look at her directly, but occupied themselves by shuffling through papers and glancing uneasily toward Bob. Amy's encouraging smile had disappeared, and she meekly stared at the papers in front of her. Even Jed's angry demeanor had faded and he now looked subdued.

Attempting to reign in his apprehension, Bob began to speak again. "I have invited you all to this meeting because you have been chosen for placement on The Company Website Team." As he said that, it occurred to him that Priscilla had not participated in the evaluations. *Why is she here? Does The Manager feel that the team needs to be supervised? Or is it maybe that I in particular need to be supervised?* He couldn't imagine proceeding with her there to perhaps judge and criticize his every move. Still, team leadership was certainly unfamiliar territory for him, so maybe some supervision was in order. Also, he hadn't been with The Company as long as she had, and he certainly didn't have her education and skills, let alone her status in The Company. *So, Bob, maybe now it's time to admit you have no business being on this team, let alone leading it. No, I am not going to go there again! The Manager has clearly indicated that he is pleased to have me lead this group. Therefore I will trust him with that decision. I don't understand why he sent Priscilla, but I am not going to worry, and I am going to do this to the best of my ability. If I have problems I will simply talk it over with him, and he will help me.*

His silence as he paused to think had not gone unnoticed, and in particular Priscilla had started to tap a pen on the table as she stared impatiently at him. He had no doubt she had important work waiting for her, so he forced a slight smile at her and continued speaking. "First, I would like to share with you all just a bit of the vision for the website that comes from The Manager." For the next few minutes Bob addressed how The Manager's vision would be translated overall into the content of the website. Although he was not at all accustomed to speaking publicly, he found his nervousness began to dissipate as he focused on the subject of his speech.

Then it was time to discuss who would have what role on the team. Of course it would be based primarily on ability and skill sets. As he looked up from his agenda and focused on those present, he realized it might be unwise to try to continue without at least acknowledging the misgivings of some. He cleared his throat and said, "I'd like to share some things with you before we talk about the assigning of specific roles. I am aware that not all of you are happy with me as The Manager's choice to lead this group. You consider me to be unqualified, and in some respects you may be right about that. I certainly don't have the training and skills that a lot of you in this room have. In fact, I came into The Company lacking any formal training and skill for any sort of work here. I worked as a dishwasher at a diner downtown before I came here. But as you all are aware, The Manager doesn't hire on the basis of our qualifications."

He paused momentarily as he wondered just how much truth about himself he should reveal. It felt like the right thing to do, however, and so he continued, "Over time I started to take the wonderful, undeserved opportunity I'd been given for granted, and I started to become weary in my work. I won't now talk about how difficult the work was at times, nor will I talk about how some coworkers were uncooperative and maybe even treated me unfairly at times. And I will not talk about how people outside The Company can often be a source of discouragement. Because you see, I can't use any of those things as excuses. Focusing on whether or not work was fair only led to my becoming even more lazy and unproductive. The more unfair it seemed, the more justified I felt in my poor choices, and eventually my weariness and preoccupation with myself and my own problems led to my completely giving up. I actually went outside and took a nap – yep, fell asleep on the grass. I had a dream, a nightmare really, which was all about my having left my work unattended, and the havoc that ensued. Well, I woke up and found out it was more than a mere dream. Because I actually had left things unattended there were some very real consequences. I won't try to explain it beyond that.

"Thankfully, The Manager wasn't intent on firing me. Since that time, he has made me realize that he isn't going to give up on me as his employee, in spite of my failures. I think we all know that he's that way with all of us! I am exceedingly thankful for his grace, and I have totally recommitted myself to him, to The Company, and to my work. I've been daily spending time in the Employee Manual like when I first started, and I've been learning and growing a lot as an employee. I have to tell you that I'm happier now than even when I first started here.

"I tell you these things to assure you that I understand how you may not consider me a very good fit for the leadership of this team. But I've been learning some things about The Manager's perspective. Although it's true I do have some proficiency in website construction, he clearly didn't make me the team leader because I had the highest level of expertise. I've found that he values our character more than a job done perfectly. He values our willingness and availability even more than our abilities and knowledge. I'm sure you all remember what he said at the conclusion of the evaluations; that he made me the leader because I talked to him to find out what he really wanted regarding the website team, and because of my concern for the others who might be beneficial to have on the team, but couldn't be considered for placement without a little help and training. Most of all, I believe he made me the leader because I have a profound respect for him, and a renewed desire to please him above my own aspirations. Even when I told him that I was not sure I could lead the team, he said he had confidence that with help from him, I could. You see, it's not really about our own ability apart from The Manager, it's about accomplishing all that he wants done with his help.

"Because my desire is to please him, and because he has entrusted this role to me, I am committed to putting forth my best effort as the team leader, no matter what some of you in this room may think. For this team to be successful, I need everyone on the team to be as wholehearted and cooperative as possible. So, if you're ready to trust The Manager in his decision to have me lead the team, and ready to set aside your own agenda and focus on what's good for the team as well as The Manager's vision for the website, then I welcome you to this team. But if you are not willing for any reason, I will not blame or criticize you, that's between you and The Manager, and you are free to go back to your work."

Bob knew that Priscilla had been staring at him intently throughout his speech, and he now gathered the courage to look back at her for more than a fleeting second. What he saw surprised him. Her haughty expression had been replaced by one of near shock. He hoped he hadn't somehow offended her, and he wondered once again why she was even in the room. For the sake of getting on with the meeting, he focused on the rest of the group. They all looked somewhat dazed. Jed looked as surprised as the rest, but beyond that, Bob couldn't read his expression.

He sat back down and looked over the agenda before saying, "So, I have role assignments for the team, but if you are not inclined to continue, again I say that you are free to leave." It only took a few minutes to explain his choices for the team positions. No one voiced any disagreement, and no one left the room. Bob wondered if the speech he had just given had helped to appease those who were inclined to be contentious, or if perhaps it had simply left everyone too stunned to react.

He looked again at Priscilla, and as he did so, she slowly and deliberately stood up. Unsmiling, she stared at Bob and said tersely, "Well! I am sure you will let me know if there is anything you need." With her head held high and heels clicking, she made her exit. Puzzled by her statement, Bob made a mental note to talk to The Manager. *A simple question, really. Why was she in the room?* That's all he felt he needed to know. He fielded a few questions from his new team members, and then breathed a shaky sigh of relief as the last one left the room. He had gotten through leading his first team meeting. It felt monumental.

Immediately after the meeting, Bob dropped his paperwork off in his office and quickly checked for voice and email messages. There was nothing urgent, so he then went straight to The Manager's office. After a bit of talk about the meeting in general, he asked his simple question about Priscilla.

The Manager looked thoughtful for a moment and then explained, "I asked Priscilla to help you with things like making copies if you need them. As my personal assistant, she has in her office one of the best copy machines in the building. She's also good at scheduling things, catering for example, for when you have a lunch meeting planned."

Bob was stunned. "She's your assistant? You asked her to help us with things like food and copies?"

The Manager smiled. "She should have told you. She knows what I asked her to do."

Bob stared at him in bewilderment, but The Manager didn't look too concerned. His desk phone rang, and he said with an encouraging smile, "We're done here for now, Bob. So go on, and do your work faithfully and sensibly."

Later that day, Bob stepped out into the hallway and looked in both directions before heading toward the main offices again. He wanted to explain to The Manager that something about the email he had just received from Priscilla was fishy. He stopped after a few hesitant steps, however. *Maybe I should look at that email one more time before I trouble The Manager. Maybe I'm being hasty. Maybe it's not as bad as it seemed.* He headed back into his office, and then indecisively he headed back out into the hallway again where he stood still to think. *Didn't The Manager say he's always there for me? Do I have to be literally hanging from the face of a cliff for that to be true?* He sighed in frustration. *Okay, okay, one more time, look at the email. I'm sure there is nothing to panic about here.*

Returning once again to his desk, he reopened and reread the email. *Less than friendly would be an understatement. And this is so unfair to Amy. She must be struggling as she deals with this right now. But The Manager tells me not to worry, ever, about anything.* As he stared at the email, Bob thought about what The Manager had said in regard to the support he had asked Priscilla to provide for the team. *From this email, you'd think he asked her to manage the team herself! But he didn't, he asked her to make copies and schedule catering! She has no excuse for treating Amy and me like this! I definitely need to talk to The Manager!*

As he was once more signing out of his email there was a light knock on his door. The thought occurred to him that it could actually be The Manager, who of course would already be aware of any problems he might be having. He eagerly jumped up from his desk and opened the door. It was not The Manager.

"Bob, I have some things to say to you."

As if trouble with Priscilla isn't enough, now I have to deal with Jed? Okay, I'll just explain that I really don't have time for this...

"First, I want to say I'm sorry. Will you forgive me for the way I acted in your meeting this morning?"

Surprised and confused, Bob stared silently at him. *Jed is asking me to forgive him? He's not trying to cause more trouble?*

Before he could think what to say, Jed explained, "You see, as I'm sure you know, I was one of the ones who was not happy to have you lead the team. I thought The Manager had made a huge mistake. But after your talk I did some thinking, and you were right about a lot of things. I've been regressing in my own attitudes lately, and feeling like my work here was not really appreciated. I was feeling sorry for myself and developing a strong resistance to the ways of The Company and even The Manager himself. I also have to confess that I was jealous of your promotion to the spot of team leader. I felt like I deserved it more than you did. But with your speech, you broke the resistance I have been allowing to build up against everything I once knew to be right. So, I did some serious thinking, and then I went and had a talk with The Manager. Now I'm here to apologize and to thank you for helping me to see the truth about myself, and also for offering me the opportunity to be on your team." When Bob continued to stare speechlessly at him, he added, "And I would also like to say that I will do my best to help you create a great website."

It finally dawned on Bob that not only was Jed smiling sincerely, his uniform was spotlessly white. "Are you serious?"

Jed extended his hand to shake Bob's. "Very serious."

Bob returned his handshake enthusiastically and said, "Jed, that's great! Of course I accept your apology, and I'm happy to have you on the team! We really need your expertise, and I'm looking forward to working with you!"

"I'm looking forward to working with you as well. And there's something else I want to tell you, something that I already told The Manager. I admire the way you handled the meeting. First, you had unhappy employees including myself to deal with, and then Priscilla showed up. I could tell you were uneasy about her being there, as were we all, but you handled the entire meeting with confidence and a straightforward plan. The Manager says he's proud of you!"

"Wow, thanks! It was a bit of a challenge, that's for sure! I actually was hoping it might be The Manager just now knocking at my door. I'm still having some trouble with Priscilla and I guess I'm not sure how to handle it."

"Hmmm. Have you gone to Priscilla and talked to her directly about the situation?"

Bob winced inwardly as he remembered past interactions with Priscilla. What came to mind most painfully was her sharp tongue and disdainful attitude. Although he knew he shouldn't allow himself to feel intimidated by her, he felt somewhat helpless about it. After all, she had been an employee of The Company for a long time, and had even received commendations and promotions from The Manager. Even now that Bob knew she wasn't really a manager it was still difficult to think of her as just another employee.

"Well, no," he finally said. "Not really sure I want to talk to her at all."

"Yeah, I know she can be difficult. I've had a few run-ins with her myself. But there are some things we both have to remember – she is your coworker, a fellow employee, and therefore just as important to The Manager and to The Company as you and I. It would likely be good to cut her some slack, be patient, and forgive her. You know, I find it helpful in times like this to remember everything The Manager has forgiven me for."

Bob nodded. "Yeah, you're sure right about that." As he thought, some other things The Manager had told him recently came to mind. *You woke up and came to your senses, and you have changed your direction. However, you need to be aware that your situation has not changed. Work will still be difficult. You will still have daily challenges. But you must remember that your coworkers are also my employees. They have difficulties and challenges, just as you do, and often they are dealing with things you will not even be aware of that could make them less than easy to work with. For their sake, for your own sake, for my sake and for the sake of The Company, I want you to forgive and remain friendly in all situations.*

"Jed, there's something else about the situation which makes it even more difficult, and that is that someone else is involved. I just hate to see this other person not being treated with – well, kindness and respect, I guess."

Jed thought for a moment and then said, "Perhaps it would be a good idea to take that other person with you when you talk to Priscilla." Suddenly his cell phone rang. After a quick glance at it he said, "Well, I gotta take this. Let me know if I can be of any help, okay?" As he started to walk away he asked, "Hey, you want to grab lunch together sometime?"

"Sure, that would be great!" As Bob walked back into his office, he realized he had just made a new friend. This was especially appealing because of late his friendships had been dwindling. The malcontents he used to hang out with didn't get his renewed commitment, and even avoided him. Jed on the other hand now had a renewed enthusiasm similar to his own, and Bob couldn't help but feel a special connection to him. He also felt grateful for the good advice Jed had just given him, and he decided to talk to Amy to see if she would be willing to accompany him to talk with Priscilla.

Chapter 12

A short time later, Bob was in Amy's office discussing the email they had both received from Priscilla. One other person had received a copy of the email, and that was Becky, the head of The Company's Graphic Design Department. Bob had just invited Amy to go along with him to have a conciliatory conversation with Priscilla.

With a disheartened look, Amy replied, "Bob, I can't talk to Priscilla about this. Actually I can't talk to Priscilla about much of anything. The weather, maybe. Come to think of it, she never even agrees with me about the weather. I'm always wrong with her even on simple stuff, and it's like nothing I do ever really deserves any credit, or it's not good enough somehow as far as she's concerned. And what she said in the email about me not deserving to have a position on the website team, especially as lead graphic designer, well, what am I going to say to her about that? Nothing. Because she's right. You know yourself I don't have the skills and training like Becky has, just as Priscilla pointed out."

Bob tried to protest, but Amy ignored him and kept talking. "But they have no right to be mean to me about it. Do you know how awful it feels to have someone say you are no good at something, especially if it's something you love to do? And to have the two of them talking about you behind your back? Well, it feels awful. Priscilla says I will never be successful in graphic design unless I take all the years of training like Becky, and then spend years practicing. That's not something I have time or inclination for. And the thing is that even if I did all that like she says I should, I still don't think she would ever accept me as being good enough. And for you to say we should go to her office and be nice to her, and try to talk to her about this, well, I don't know."

Amy suddenly sat back in her chair and eyed Bob sharply. "Maybe you're on their side, and you're regretting that you put me on the team in the first place. Maybe you should just do what she says and replace me with Becky as the lead designer for the team." Amy finally stopped talking, and her expression dared Bob to disagree with her.

"No, Amy, it's not that I agree with them and no way am I on their side in their attitudes about this. There's a part of me that would love to punch them both in the snoot for you!"

Amy's expression softened, and then she laughed. "You would do that for me?"

Bob smiled, but then he said, "Well, yes I would, but you know I can't, and even allowing myself to think that way isn't going to help either one of us."

Amy sighed. "Well, you're probably right, but I still can't talk to Priscilla."

Bob thought for a moment, and then said resignedly, "Okay then, I will talk to her myself. Maybe I can get this resolved without you having to be there."

Amy agreed thankfully, and Bob returned to his office and once again opened the email. Making a quick decision, he printed out the message, folded it and jammed it into a pocket before heading to Priscilla's office.

Once there, it didn't take much conversing with her for Bob to reach the limit of his patience. In exasperation, he pulled the paper out of his pocket. "Look, this is what you said! This is the email you sent me not even an hour ago!"

Rigidly, Priscilla glanced at the email and then replied, "So? You know yourself Amy is not qualified for that position. In fact, I really don't understand why The Manager let you be responsible for the website team in the first place, because you aren't qualified either!" She gave Bob a withering and triumphant look before saying, "And I really don't have time for this. I have important work to do, nothing you would know anything about." With a dismissive shrug, she turned back to her computer.

Bob's final shred of control snapped and he found himself lashing out at her. "You were supposed to help out with this project! You've done nothing to help, nothing whatsoever! You know what? I don't need your kind of help, and neither does Amy! You are completely worthless!" He then turned and stormed out of her office.

Although his pace leaving her office was brisk, he shortly stopped in his tracks altogether and mulled the situation over. *Bob you're a dope! You knew she wasn't likely to listen or to be pleasant! And yet once again, here you are! You've lost your temper and failed again! How could you yell at The Manager's own assistant? Maybe this was your last chance and now The Manager will fire you for sure!*

Even as his thoughts accused him, he determinedly resisted them, standing a little straighter as he did so. *The Manager's not going to fire me. He won't be pleased that I didn't control my temper, but he's not going to fire me. He would want me to try again.* Bob gritted his teeth. A few moments ago all he had to do was maintain his composure. Now he had to go back, and not only talk to her again, but apologize first.

As he slowly started to head back to her office a thought suddenly occurred to him. Although the website project was important, he also had another project with an even greater urgency and impending deadline. It was getting late in the day, and it certainly would do no good to leave that project unfinished. Maybe tomorrow would be a better day to try again to talk to Priscilla. Although as he hastened to his office he felt relieved to have an irrefutable excuse to put off apologizing, he also had an uneasy sense of foreboding.

A few days later, Bob stood quietly in The Manager's office while The Manager stood behind his desk studying a report he held. Bob knew exactly what The Manager was seeing for himself, and that was that the report was incomplete and past its due date.

The Manager finally looked up and asked quietly, "Bob, I trusted you to finish this report on the progress of the website team. Would you like to tell me what happened?"

Bob wondered if the big screen behind The Manager would suddenly flicker to life if he failed to reveal the entire truth of the matter. *Still, what can I say about Priscilla?* "Sir, I apologize. And I want to tell you the truth. I had a fairly good start on the report, but then I had issues with Priscilla over management of the team. I tried to talk to her about our disagreement, but it didn't go well, and I lost my temper and left her office. I was going to go back to apologize to her and try to talk to her again, but then I remembered that other project, the one you needed done right away, so I went back to my office and worked on that, and the next day I kept working on that project until it was finished. Then I thought again about going to apologize to Priscilla, but I knew it was going to be difficult to talk to her, especially since I had to apologize first for losing my temper, so while I was thinking about it I opened an internet game. I played games for a while. When I closed the games, I checked my messages, and there was some work that I needed to do. Before I knew it the day was nearly over, and so I told myself again I would go tomorrow and apologize." Bob's voice finally trailed off. He felt dismal as he stood still and waited for The Manager's response.

The Manager was quiet for a few moments, and then said, "Bob, I have seen your sincere efforts of late to please me, and I know right now you are feeling discouraged because here you are yet again, having to confess your failures. I want you to know that I am sympathetic, and as always, I forgive you. Still, we need to talk through this. So tell me. Do you blame Priscilla for your failure to complete the assignment? Or do you suppose that the problem here is the internet gaming itself?"

Bob thought soberly. *The internet games are certainly distracting at times. And how do you offer criticism about one who seems to be so favored by The Manager?* He decided to focus on the internet games. "Well, it's certainly a temptation to play games instead of working sometimes, especially when I'm struggling with problems. Maybe the best thing would be to remove the game apps from my computer, maybe even block the internet gaming somehow." As he spoke, he couldn't help but feel regretful. *Maybe I wouldn't have to give up the games if I'd just kept it for legitimate break times.* He waited quietly, preparing himself for whatever decision The Manager would make.

"Bob, taking away all freedom of choice about such things might seem to be the right answer, for yourself and for all of my employees. It's possible that would have the effect of my employees finishing more work in a timely fashion. The reasons for my not doing that are a bit complicated. Part of it is that I certainly do care about you and I want you to be happy. Having something you enjoy doing for fun now and then cannot automatically be classified as bad. Even more importantly, my allowing you freedom to choose also has to do with your growth and maturity as my employee. Learning to make right choices especially when the choices are difficult is a very important part of growth."

The Manager paused, and then seemed to change the subject as he said, "You have been spending time lately quietly reading the Employee Manual with a desire to absorb it as fully as possible. So, tell me, is the Manual merely a book of lessons and instructions teaching you all about how to get the work itself done, or is there more to it than that?"

"Well, it does teach about accomplishing the work of course, but there is a lot more to it than just that. It's really more about training in attitudes and dispositions and character development and stuff like that."

"Yes. Apparently I care about who you are as an individual even more than I care about the work itself, wouldn't you agree?"

"Yes. Every other company I know of has the end result of the work itself as its highest priority. It's taken me a long time to realize it, and I'm still not sure I fully understand it, but you place a higher priority on your workers than on the finished work. You value and care for your employees in a way I have never seen in any other manager."

"Because I care about you, I value giving you time for refreshing breaks, and time to simply enjoy life within The Company. Choices, however, come with consequences. One of my highest priorities is to see you grow beyond making choices based solely on the fear of consequences, or even on the hope of reward. It's helpful to recognize there are consequences, and it's also good to remember and be encouraged by knowing my reward for your work is real. You will not be disappointed with your ultimate hope of tomorrow. Still, my goal is that you mature into one who has a sincere desire to do the right and courageous thing even when faced with difficult choices. My goal is that you become one who trusts me enough to choose the difficult path when it is the right path regardless of consequences or rewards."

After a thoughtful pause, The Manager continued, "Who you are is far more important to me than what you do. But the truth also is that ultimately what you do will prove who you are. Your identity as my employee gives you vision. As you grow and mature, you will value faithfulness and persistence more than playing games. Your choices will reflect your values."

The Manager paused thoughtfully, his eyes toward the floor. When he looked again at Bob he said, "So, the Employee Manual is about more than just how to do the work. It's about values and principles, and training in character development. Is that all? Have we talked about the very most important aspect of it?"

Bob considered the question carefully before he replied, "It's really most of all about getting to know you. It's about your character and who you are as my Manager. It's about your relationship with all of your employees, me included."

"Bob, you are learning the reality and value of our relationship. I will not abandon you, not ever. You will become fully faithful, just as I am faithful to you. Now let's move on. Bob, why do you suppose Priscilla dresses up and does not wear the standard uniform?"

Bob cleared his throat a bit nervously. "Well, I believe it's because she's special somehow in The Company. I know now she's not a high level manager or anything like I thought before, so I guess she has special permission to dress up all fancy like she does because she's your assistant."

"All this guessing!" The Manager smiled and shook his head slightly. "I'm going to tell you some things about Priscilla because you need to understand. In a significant way, Priscilla started out in The Company differently than you did. She struggled with some things you did not because she had a background unlike yours. She was well educated and had outstanding credentials. She could have gone to work for pretty much any company she chose. Unlike many, Priscilla actually studied her options and made a decision to seek out employment in The Company. When she talked to me and realized she could not be hired on the basis of her own achievements, that she had to set aside her distinguished past with all of her honors and accolades, she went home to think it over. She made her decision and came back to accept my offer of employment in The Company based purely on my grace. She started off dressed every day in a pure white uniform, just as you did. She spent time in the Employee Manual trying to draw from it everything she needed to be a good employee. She appreciated the help she received from those who had been here longer. I have to say that she grew very fast as a productive employee, humbly seeking to please me as her Manager. Her sincere effort and accomplishment is what led me to promote her to the role of my personal assistant."

The Manager paused thoughtfully before he continued, "But, like you, she gradually became tired in her work, especially because she felt like it wasn't always noticed. Her memories of her own illustrious past began to subtly draw her back into the desire to be recognized for her own personal accomplishments. She began to feel that giving up her personal success to work for The Company might have been too great a price to pay after all. Additionally, when she was praised for her good work here in the Company, rather than accept the praise humbly, she began to think of it as her due. Worst of all, she began to consider herself to be more exceptional than all of her coworkers. She imagined her talents to be uniquely superior, and she began to yearn to be seen by the others as influential in a singular way that they themselves could never achieve. With her declining attitudes came the graying of her uniform, something you understand quite well. So, you see, she could no longer dress the same as everyone else in the standard uniform. She felt she had to do something to distinguish herself as well as to remove the guilty stains. Hence, the fancy clothes and jewelry."

Bob's eyebrows were raised in surprise. "Wow. I really thought it was because she was – well, you know, special and important to you somehow."

"Bob, you need to know that I have the same care for all of my employees. You are all very special and important to me. I favor all of my employees and yet I do not play favoritism."

"Sir, I knew somehow that I shouldn't let myself feel intimidated by her, but I think she makes a lot of us feel intimidated and incompetent by comparison."

"Yes, I am aware of the way she is perceived by others. That does not at all mean I approve of lofty attitudes, not in her, nor in any of you. As you mature in my employ, you will learn not to entertain feelings of inferiority. It's not helpful to compare yourself to your coworkers, but instead look to me for your sense of worth in The Company. I value true humility, not feelings of superiority, nor feelings of inferiority. It's very important to me that you know who you are, and that you feel secure in your identity as my employee."

After a pause, The Manager continued, "When you are feeling intimidated, please consider that because my employees are at different points on their journey of life within The Company, you will always encounter imperfection. At times, people will seek you out for reasons which are only beneficial to themselves. They may even try to get you to use your time and talents for their own agendas. They will likely have superior attitudes and may even assert that their agenda is the only one that matters. Instead of yielding to intimidating spirits, simply remember whose employee you are, and who signs your paycheck."

With his new understanding, Bob suddenly had a sense of compassion for Priscilla. "So, is she destined to stay that way? I mean, can she ever get back to being happy just to be one of your employees like the rest of us?"

The Manager smiled. "Were you destined to remain lazy and ineffective in your own work?"

"Uh, no. I see what you mean. If she turns around, if she wakes up, she can come back too."

"That's exactly right. Although I certainly don't approve of her choices and attitudes, I am allowing her the freedom to dress and behave the way she does, and I patiently keep the door open for her to turn around when she's ready to stop running from her own destiny."

After a thoughtful pause, The Manager redirected the conversation. "Bob, I have two questions for you to ask yourself and consider as you go about your work today. First, why do you say 'tomorrow'? Second, what does 'freedom' mean to you? Also, when you go back to apologize to Priscilla, I would like you to ask her if there is anything that she could use your help with."

Bob stared blankly at The Manager for a moment, then he asked slowly, "So, you want me to go back and not only apologize, but try to see if there's some way I can help her, even though she's the one who is supposed to be helping me with copies and stuff?"

The Manager smiled. "I'm not saying that she deserves it. You would be going the extra mile, but I would truly appreciate it."

Bob grimaced for a moment, but then he drew himself up and said, "Sir, this doesn't feel easy. But I've been giving a lot of thought to all that you have done for me. You've given me grace way beyond what I could have earned or deserved in any way. And I've been thinking about the things you said about me being your representative or ambassador as your employee. I'm beginning to understand that it isn't about my needs or wants, but it's about representing you and The Company. And I got upset with Priscilla because she offended both me and Amy as well, but I wasn't there to represent myself in the first place. I'm beginning to understand that as your ambassador, what you would do in a situation is what I should do. I have to learn to put you and The Company above my own personal feelings and goals."

"Good! And what do you think I would have done in the situation?"

Bob smiled. "Well, you sure wouldn't have lost your temper like I did!" He thoughtfully added, "I think you would have been patient, and then you would have offered to help her, like you're asking me to do. But I do think she would have treated you with more respect in the first place." Bob hoped his last statement didn't sound defensive.

The Manager chuckled. "You would be surprised at the way some of my employees feel more or less entitled to treat me. But yes, she likely would have behaved more respectfully toward me. Still, for my sake, will you talk to her again with these things in mind?"

"Yes Sir, I will."

A short time later, Bob found himself in Priscilla's office. The apology came out more easily than he had feared, but it only took a minute, and then he stood still, wondering what to say next. He had a fleeting thought that he ought to show her who the real boss of the website team was by telling her to schedule food for a lunch meeting. *Careful here, don't regress into childish, spiteful behavior. Cut her some slack!*

As Priscilla stared back at him, Bob could see she was stunned and speechless at his apology. He took a deep breath and asked calmly, "So, how is your day going, Priscilla? Is there perhaps something I can help you with?"

For a moment her bewilderment grew, but then she quickly regained her composure. With a toss of her hair, she gestured toward a stack of binders on a table. "I need those copied. You'll have to take each document out of each binder, make ten copies of each one, get more binders from Supplies and put the copies in them, and deliver a complete set of bound copies to each individual listed here." With a flourish she handed him a list of ten names. "And I need that all done and delivered by the end of the day." Without waiting for a response, she quickly turned and busied herself on her computer.

Steeling himself to keep The Manager's directives at heart, Bob silently picked up the stack. Yet, as he walked away from her office, his thoughts assailed him. *Now she thinks I'm a wimp, just her whipping boy. She'll be after me every day to do stuff like this for her. She'll treat me like a slave from here on out, and everyone will see it and laugh at me. I'll never get any of my own work done because I'll be too busy…*

"Stop it," he chided himself out loud. "Trust The Manager!"

The rest of his day went by quickly. His task for Priscilla took less time than he had feared, allowing him the time he needed to make phone calls and respond to emails in regard to his own assignments. Later that afternoon he set out to deliver the copied documents. Although he received a few questions as to why he was delivering copies usually delivered by Priscilla, he found it not too difficult to give a simple answer. "The Manager asked me to give her a hand today, that's all." A couple of individuals gave him a smirking stare, but again, he steadied himself. *It doesn't matter what they think. Let it go, don't dwell on it.*

Soon he was back in his office, finishing up some work before heading home for the night. Then it dawned on him then that he had not yet returned the original documents to Priscilla. It was certainly an easy task, but not one he looked forward to simply because he didn't relish more interaction with her. *Maybe tomorrow will be soon enough to return them to her.* Immediately he knew that was not the right attitude as he thought again about The Manager's questions for him earlier. *Why do you say, 'tomorrow'? What does 'freedom' mean to you?* He knew the only appropriate choice was to take the originals to her right away. She must be wondering whether or not he had even completed the task.

Shortly he was in her office, dropping off the documents. "Hi Priscilla, here are your original documents. They're all copied, bound and delivered to the people on this list." He placed the stack on the table with the list resting on top of it.

She glanced at him briefly and replied, "Thanks," before turning back to her computer.

Although he felt she could have shown a little more gratitude, at least she wasn't handing him a 'next assignment,' so he thought it good to make a quick exit. "You're welcome," he said, and headed out the door.

As he was leaving, he passed Becky, the head of the Graphic Design Department, as she was on her way in to see Priscilla. He nodded politely as he continued walking down the hall. Shortly he heard two sets of high heels clicking on the tile floor, so he turned and briefly watched Priscilla and Becky walking together in the other direction. He suddenly realized that Becky was not wearing the standard uniform and wondered when she had started dressing up the way Priscilla did. It occurred to him that a lesson could be learned from their behavior. Perhaps the worst thing about becoming weary and complacent in your own work was that you tended to negatively influence other employees, something that could possibly even lead to their own giving up. He made a mental commitment to be careful whenever he felt weary himself so that he might not become a discouragement to any coworker who might be struggling just to hang on.

Chapter 13

As Bob walked slowly to Amy's office, he thought about his reasons for this visit. He really wanted to encourage her and tell her not to worry about the criticism and dissuasion she had received from Priscilla and Becky. He wanted her to just come along and enjoy being a part of the website team, and embrace the opportunity to use her talents in graphic design. But he also knew there was something much more important at stake than merely whether or not she should be the team's lead graphic designer. Of late he had noticed that her uniform was beginning to gray just as his own had done before he had given up and taken the nap. He was concerned and wanted to help her, but he also knew The Manager was the only one who could really help her. *But having that talk with The Manager has to be her own choice. And I don't want to sound judgmental, so maybe I should just not say anything. Still, if there is any way to help her...*

The door to Amy's office was ajar, so Bob pushed it open and quietly walked in. Her back was toward him as she worked at something on her computer. After watching her for a few moments, he asked, "Hey Amy, whatcha up to?"

Startled, she jumped slightly and turned toward him. "Bob, don't scare me like that!"

He could see as she turned around that she had actually been playing a video game. "Sorry, the door was open. So, what game you playing?"

Amy sighed as she turned back to her computer. "It's just online poker with animation. I just lost to the monkey again, so the crowd is booing me."

Bob laughed. "Wow, just what you need when you lose, right?"

"Yeah, like that crowd could do any better!" Amy closed the game window and opened a folder of graphic files. "I suppose you'd like to see my ideas for the website. I haven't really done much, I'm just experimenting with some possible designs, you know, for if I actually end up doing any design work for the site."

"If you do any design work for the site! Amy, you know I need you on the team!"

Amy surveyed Bob with skepticism before she replied, "Hasn't Priscilla convinced you Becky should have that role?"

"Priscilla is not in charge of the team, I am. Priscilla is going to make copies for us when we need them, and set up catering if we have a lunch meeting. Becky didn't indicate an interest in being on the team in the first place by participating in the evaluations, and she already has plenty of design work to do for The Company anyway. But besides all that, I picked you! I think you can handle it!"

Amy looked puzzled. "Priscilla's going to make copies and schedule catering for us? Why would she do that?"

Bob smiled understandingly but spoke cautiously as he silently reminded himself to be respectful. "Priscilla is The Manager's personal assistant. He asked her to help out the team with those kinds of administrative tasks."

Amy stared at Bob in amazement, then finally asked, "So, why all the fancy clothes and attitude? I thought she was a manager of some kind. I think everybody thinks that."

"Yep, I know, but she really is just what I said. So, let's not worry about her. Let's think about how you can make our website look fabulous, okay?" Amy appeared to be mulling over this new information about Priscilla and didn't respond, so Bob added, "Amy, I really think this is a good opportunity for you. I'd hate to see you not take advantage of it. I really feel you would be missing out on something very special."

With a weary sigh, Amy replied, "Well, maybe. But the thing is, it seems like every time I get all revved up about something, and I put a lot of time and effort into it, something goes wrong, and there's trouble. I'm tired of trouble. Maybe if I stopped trying so hard, the trouble would go away. Maybe if I didn't care so much about work, I'd find out it wasn't all that important anyway. Besides that, I don't really know for sure design work for the website is something I'm all that capable of doing. But if I don't pursue it, then I can't fail, you see what I mean?" She eyed Bob sharply.

"Well, I suppose it's true that you can't fail if you don't try at something, but I don't see how not trying is better than trying even if you don't end up succeeding. Besides, I don't believe at all that you will fail, I believe you will succeed. I've seen some of your design work, and you are talented! Above all that, The Manager helps us with everything. He would look out for you and even make sure of your success."

Amy seemed to consider what he said for a moment, but then sighed again and replied, "I guess so, but I just don't feel like I have the energy for the commitment it would take. I don't feel inspired somehow, or motivated. I just feel tired."

"Amy, how can you say you're not inspired? You've already been trying out designs!"

"Yes, I manage to squeeze in a few minutes of design work between playing games and checking on my blog, which, by the way, I also feel uninspired about. I haven't posted anything new for a month, not sure why I was even looking at it. It's depressing!" As she spoke, she stood up and looked out the window. "Bob, have you ever noticed how many meadowlarks there are around here? Don't they sound pretty?"

Oh no! Not the meadowlarks! Next she'll be headed out of here looking for a quiet place to take a nap!

"Amy, I know the birds sound pretty, but listen to me. I know sometimes it seems hard, but you can't give up. Think about how much the Manager cares about you, and how sad he would be if you gave up."

Amy's eyes suddenly welled up with tears and she reached for a tissue. "He doesn't care about me. This wouldn't be so hard if he cared about me! Things wouldn't be so unfair!" She wiped away the tears that were spilling over and then blew her nose.

"Come on Amy, you know he cares about us more than we can even know! He values us in a way I've never seen in any other manager. We aren't just workers to him; he truly cares about each one of us individually! And even though things seem unfair sometimes, ultimately he works things out for us and they turn out to be so much better than just fair. Just think about the retirement package we are promised; have you ever heard of anything even close to that kind of retirement from any other company?"

"That's another thing! How do we even know for sure that the retirement package is for real? I mean when you think about it, the entire Company retiring together and spending forever with The Manager, and everyone is happy and everything is perfect and there are never any problems or troubles, and well, you know, how do we know for sure because sometimes it sounds too good to be true?"

"Amy, the reason I believe all that to be true is that The Manager himself told us about it. My beliefs about retirement are based on everything I have come to believe about him. I believe he is true and faithful. He has said we will not be disappointed about the reward and retirement he has planned for us, and I believe him. Sometimes just thinking about retirement is what gets me through the difficult days here!"

Amy was silent for a few moments, then said, "Somehow I guess I still do believe all that too, but I feel like I've messed up, and I don't know how to get back to the way things were before. I feel guilty every time I see The Manager, even though he talks kindly to me." Her voice trailed off and she sat quietly before suddenly asking, "Bob, about that speech you gave in the website meeting – did you really mean all of it? You know, about waking up, and about being happier now than when you first started?"

"Yes, I meant all of it."

"And your uniform – it's white now, like when you first started." She looked down at her own uniform and brushed futilely at the discolored sleeves.

"Yes, mine is white again. You know there's only one way to get it white again."

"Yes, I know. I have to talk to The Manager and tell him everything, and ask him to forgive me." She turned and stared out the window for a moment before she looked back at Bob and asked, "When you went to talk to The Manager, did you see the angel? Did an angel talk to you?"

"Yes."

"Did the angel ask if you were ready to tell The Manager the truth?"

"Yes, he did."

"And did you? Did you tell The Manager the truth?"

"Yes I did. It wasn't easy, but I admitted to all of my failures, my lies and laziness, and not getting my work done, and leaving my office unattended. And I admitted I didn't go take a nap on a hill because I was sleepy, but because I felt burned out and I wanted to give up. So, I'm guessing that if you're asking me that question, you've seen the angel too. Did he ask you if you were ready to tell The Manager the truth?"

"Yes," Amy replied sadly, "I told the angel I was ready to tell The Manager the truth, but when I got into his office, I just couldn't do it. I guess I wasn't ready after all. And I haven't been back to talk to him like that since. Oh, we talk. He asks about work, if everything is going okay and all that everyday stuff. But we don't talk about – well, you know."

"But you could talk about it! He's the only one who can help you get back to where you want to be in your heart!" Bob was suddenly interrupted by a ring from his cell phone. Pulling it out of his pocket and giving it a quick glance, he said, "Amy, I've got some work I have to do now, it can't wait. Will you please think this over and consider going to see The Manager? Amy, you know he doesn't ever ask us to do anything that he isn't willing to help us finish. You don't have to give up like I did, you just need some encouragement!"

Amy hesitated and then said, "I know you are right. I really don't want to be like this. I can't exist here at The Company this way, and yet at the same time there's nowhere else to go." Deep in thought, Amy stared at the floor. Finally she looked up and said, "Okay, I will think about talking to him." As Bob was heading out the door she added, "And Bob – thank you for caring about me."

Bob looked back at her with a big smile and said, "I do care about you, Amy! I want you to be happy here, and so does The Manager!" He felt elated as he walked down the hall. Not only had she listened to what he said, but she might even talk to The Manager!

One day a few weeks later, Bob was staring at his schedule for the day and feeling stressed. Amy had just called, and rather than tell her he was too busy right now to help her with designs for The Company website, he had said, "Sure, I'm here, come on over and I'll have a look at what you've done."

Recently he had begun to find himself busier than ever. The Manager was placing more and more confidence in him and entrusting more work and leadership to him. But he had begun to realize he was in danger of actually failing in his work if he continued trying to accomplish too much of the work by himself.

One of his biggest challenges regarding his time allocation was the overseeing of the website team. He knew he didn't need to be involved in each and every minute decision each team member had to make. Jed didn't bring every detail to him for approval; when Jed had a significant amount of work done, he would bring it to Bob for approval and together they would make any appropriate adjustments. It had occurred to Bob that if all the team members felt that confident, more would be achieved with less effort and stress on his part. After all, they were the ones with the expertise and know how. They just needed to feel empowered. It seemed an ideal solution for many reasons, not the least of which was making room in Bob's schedule for other priorities.

Rather than make a general announcement about that at a team meeting, he had simply begun to have a conversation with each individual as they brought their questions and concerns to him. "You are doing very well," he would say. "I am confident in your talents and abilities. Just go ahead and get it done, I trust you and you do not have to ask me about every detail. Don't be afraid to make mistakes, if you make a mistake, we can fix it before we actually publish it on the site." They seemed to appreciate the reassurance and encouragement. He had been putting off having that same conversation with Amy, however, and now on this particular day he had to ask himself why. Like the others, she was competent and knew far more than he did regarding the details of the design work she was doing.

He sighed as he stared at his daily planner. He had three meetings that had nothing to do with the website, some research to finish and write up in preparation for his upcoming business trip, and an important project to finish up and turn in before getting on that plane, all leaving no time to spend with Amy hashing out the colors and designs of the site pages.

So, why not just tell her that? Amy I'm too busy today to go over this stuff with you. You don't really need to rely on me so much because you know how to do this way better than I do anyway. You can handle it. I trust your judgment. He could imagine what to say, but he also imagined fearfully what her interpretation of his words might be. *I don't want to spend so much time with you. I consider you to be a nuisance. Leave me alone and let me get my own work done!*

He sighed fretfully as he heard her knock on the door. Slowly he stood up and opened the door, smiling only slightly as she entered the room.

Noting his lack of enthusiasm, she asked with concern, "Anything wrong? You look a little worried or something."

"No. I mean yes." Bob hesitated, then took a deep breath and said determinedly, "Amy, I can't do this right now." Just as he feared, her expression changed from one of concern for him to one of hurt and confusion.

"Oh! I'm sorry, I thought…" Her voice trailed off as she lowered her head and started to turn toward the door.

Quickly he reached out and gently took hold of her arm to keep her in the room. As she stared at him questioningly, he said, "Amy, I'm sorry. I should have talked to you sooner. You're doing great with your design work, and you don't need to come to me with every decision. But I didn't want to say that to you because I was afraid you might think I didn't want to spend time with you. The truth is I enjoy spending time with you, umm, a lot. It seems like more than just work. We talk and joke, and, well, I just really like being with you." Bob hesitated as he tried to read her expression. She did seem surprised, but beyond that he couldn't be sure what she was thinking. He realized he was still holding her arm, so he let go, then resolutely said, "I have a business trip. I have to get on a plane tomorrow. Today I have meetings and a project to finish. But when I get back, Amy, will you have dinner with me?"

Amy's look of confusion vanished. She smiled thoughtfully and then simply said, "Yes."

She said yes! Bob couldn't help but think that same thought over and over while on his trip. The days flew by quickly in matters related to work, but they also seemed to drag because of his desire to be on that date with Amy. But at last he found himself seated in a fancy restaurant across from her, a bit nervous and yet comfortable at the same time. It occurred to him that he had never had a relationship with any girl who seemed to respect and like him for who he really was. How could he not completely enjoy being with her?

Their first date was followed by weeks of spending more and more time together, both at work and especially during time off. They went for long walks and bike rides, caught a few movies, and had dinner together often.

Then one day, Bob was getting a tray filled in the cafeteria and looking around to see where he might sit. He saw Jed at a table in the far end of the room and thought that he probably ought to sit with him and catch up on a few details regarding the website. However, on seeing Meredith and Amy sitting together with a couple of other employees, he decided to sit with them instead. He took a seat next to Meredith and across from Amy, and shortly the three of them were engaged in casual conversation.

Although he tried to stay tuned in to the conversation, he was really thinking about the plans he and Amy had for the evening. He also couldn't help but notice how pretty she was when she smiled. That thought was somewhat disconcerting, so to cover his nervousness he decided a practical joke was in order. Pointing to something imaginary behind her, he asked with feigned alarm, "Oh my gosh, what *is* that?" Then as she turned her head to look, he sneaked a carrot stick from her plate.

Seeing nothing at all that Bob could be trying to point out, she turned back and saw that he was loudly munching the carrot stick which had been on her plate. "Hey wise guy," she scolded him playfully, "I actually was going to eat that, you know!"

Watching their antics, Meredith sighed and shook her head. "Oh for pity's sake!" she chided them with cheerful exasperation. "When are you two going to stop flirting and just get married?"

"Married!" Now unable to look at Amy, Bob kept an exaggerated look of surprise fixed on Meredith, who just shook her head and rolled her eyes. Amy giggled, which he found somewhat reassuring. At least she wasn't completely repulsed by what Meredith had said. After an awkward few moments, the trio somehow managed to return to casual conversation.

Later that same day, Bob was in The Manager's office discussing the details of a project when The Manager suddenly changed the course of the conversation. "Bob, I really appreciate what you have done for Amy. Have you noticed her white uniform and the beautiful smile on her face?"

Bob smiled and nodded enthusiastically. "Yeah, she's really turned around!"

"Yes, she certainly has. Your encouragement was exactly what she needed!

You care for her a lot, don't you Bob?"

That question caught him off guard. He wasn't sure he was ready to talk about his relationship with Amy, especially to The Manager. His thoughts raced. *And why is this so troubling to me anyway? It's because I'm not ready to admit how much I really do care for Amy, not even to myself. What would happen if I admitted my true feelings for her, what then? What if The Manager says I shouldn't spend so much time with her? What if he says our relationship is inappropriate altogether? What if he says she's actually distracting me from my work? And what if this whole thing is really some kind of trick of the adversary to make my emotions twisted and to cause me to stop focusing on The Manager and my work?*

He hadn't answered The Manager's question, and saw that he was looking at him not so much expectantly as with a hint of amusement.

Say something, stupid! "Uh, yeah, I guess I do rather like Amy." *Rather like? Open your mouth and admit that you love her!*

The Manager chuckled. "You know Bob, there is such a thing as a special kind of partnership, a team of two, if you know what I mean. Marriage among the employees of The Company is actually to be encouraged for certain couples."

Marriage! Bob's eyes widened slightly, but he remained mute.

The Manager chuckled again, then said, "Well, enough of that for now. Let's get back to the project you're working on."

For the rest of the day, Bob found it difficult to keep his mind on anything related to work at all. It seemed all he could think about was Amy and his conversation with The Manager. *Maybe I misunderstood what he said. Maybe she is a distraction, and I should stop seeing her outside of work and not spend unnecessary time with her at work. But if I do, how can I ever stop thinking about her? But The Manager said marriage is allowed, even encouraged for some couples. Are Amy and I a couple? If I told her I loved her would she think it just another joke and laugh at me? Would she think I'm being stupid? Or worse, what if she were to realize I'm serious and say, "Well Bob, I am fond of you, and I will always be your friend." Ugh. I don't think I could stand that.* Finally Bob gave his head a shake. "Okay," he said out loud. "It's time to talk to The Manager again."

This time when he entered the outer waiting room of The Manager's office, he saw the light was already green; The Manager would see him immediately. No time to even think about backing out of the conversation he planned. He took a deep breath and walked into the office.

The Manager was standing behind his desk and smiled when he saw Bob. "Four little words, Bob. "Will you marry me?" That's all you need to ask her."

Chapter 14

A s Bob boarded the plane, he couldn't help but think about Amy and the argument he'd had with her just before leaving home that morning. It hadn't been a huge argument, more of a disagreement really, but Bob was regretting that he had left without trying harder to resolve the issue. Instead he had left in a hurry, taking only a moment to plant a quick kiss on her sullen cheek and say goodbye to the kids.

Bob sighed a little gloomily. *Well, it's not like I could afford to miss my flight! Still, this rationalization is doing no good. At the very least I should have told her it will be okay, I love her and will see her in a few days, and then we will work it out together. Okay! When I find my seat I will send her a text. I'll say I'm sorry. Of course, I do have to work on that report for The Manager. Maybe I should work on that for a while first. No, text Amy first! Even The Manager would want me to do that!* He wondered what Amy was thinking, and how she would respond to his text. *If she only knew I would really rather be home with them! A Saturday morning of sleeping in and watching cartoons in our jammies together, that's what we all really need! I'd even make some pancakes for us! And sometime soon, we'll have a date night. I'll surprise Amy and get a sitter, and we'll go out and have some alone time, just the two of us! We'll try out that new restaurant downtown. It's been a long few weeks, too much work, not enough play.*

He made his way slowly down the aisle, waiting for others to find their seats and stow bags and jackets into the overhead compartments. Once his own bag was finally stowed he turned his attention to his seat, noting with some relief that he would be on the aisle. Before sitting, he glanced at the man he would be sitting next to. Startled, he looked at him again and remained standing. It was none other than his old friend, Sam.

Memories of their friendship came flooding back. Although inwardly he had forgiven Sam for the hurtful things he had said so long ago on the day they'd gone for coffee, the memory still gave him a sense of uncertainty. They had run into each other on only a couple of very brief occasions since that day, and they had both been polite but reserved. How would Sam feel now about sitting next to his old pal for the duration of the flight? Truly, it might be easier just to find an empty seat near the back of the plane. He did have to text Amy, and of course there was the report he needed to work on. Maybe he could even do some reading, or just lean back, close his eyes and rest for a while. As he thought about the choice he was suddenly faced with, he remembered some things The Manager had said to help him prepare for this trip. *Be alert. You will of course have challenges to face. You will also have to take some risks in order not to miss out on rare and eventful opportunities. Remember, it's not about your comfort. You are taking this trip to make a difference.*

Bob cleared his throat and said, "Hello Sam. Mind if I sit next to you?"

Sam took his eyes away from the view outside the plane window and stared at Bob in surprise. Regaining his composure, he shrugged and gave a slight nod toward the empty seat next to him before turning again to stare out the window.

As he sat down and fiddled with the seat belt, Bob decided to send Amy the text right away. He needed to get it done as a matter of conscience anyway, and it would give him something to do while he figured out what to say to Sam.

Sam didn't wait for Bob to speak first. Turning toward him, he said abruptly, "You're a lousy friend, you know that?"

Bob listened more to the tone of Sam's voice than his words. "Yeah, I know," he replied gently. "Sorry about that."

"Who you texting?"

"My wife. We had a bit of an argument before I left this morning."

"Something to do with the kids, no doubt."

Bob smiled slightly. "What makes you think we have kids?"

Sam shrugged. "I figured you'd be married and have kids by now. Because you know, your whole life changed when you joined The Company. Seems likely you have a lot going for you that you didn't have before."

He glanced briefly out the window again before asking, "Flying make you nervous?"

"No, not so much anymore, I guess. You?"

"Yeah, it makes me nervous! And it oughta make you nervous! Something could always go wrong on any flight, any day! It's dangerous!"

"Yes, I suppose it is."

"You seem relaxed enough. You fly often, that why you ain't nervous?"

"I've done a fair share of traveling."

"Business?"

"Mostly business." Bob didn't say more, but he knew the reasons for his lack of nervousness went beyond merely becoming used to flying.

Sam turned away and stared out the window again. When he turned back he said abruptly, "You know, I expected you to come back to the diner. I expected you to tell me that joining The Company hadn't worked out like you'd hoped, and that it was all just a big mistake. I knew our boss would take you back, not that he'd want to but he'd have to because he'd need dishwashers. I thought I'd be there to say, "Welcome back," you know, with a sort of 'told you so' attitude goin' on. By the time you did stop in for a visit, I knew that wasn't likely to happen."

Bob decided it best just to let him vent, so he nodded thoughtfully, said, "Mmhmm," and kept working on his message to Amy.

"Look, about that time we talked when you stopped in to the diner. I know what happened was a good thing for you. Thing is, it was a bad thing for me. I knew you wouldn't be hangin' out with me any more, not in the same way, not going to the bars, not ditchin' work and playin' video games all day. Felt like I'd lost my only real pal. Plus, I was jealous. You finally had it good, and my life was still goin' nowhere. I didn't know how to deal with it. I didn't know how to be glad for you when my life was still empty."

"It's okay, I understand and I'm sure I would have felt the same."

The plane had begun its taxi down the runway, and for a while neither spoke as Sam turned to stare out the window again. Then he gave Bob a pointed look and asked, "So, did you send me an invite to the weddin'?"

"I tried. It came back as undeliverable. I figured you'd moved, didn't know where to."

"Yeah, I've had a couple of lousy apartments since you left the diner."

Bob nodded as he clicked 'send' on his message and pocketed his phone. "So, where are you flying off to today?"

"Home. Gotta see Pop. He's not gonna make it much longer. This gittin' old thing's crap, ain't it?"

Bob could see that the years were taking their toll on Sam. He wanted to tell him that if would join The Company, things would be better for him. He wouldn't even fear getting older so much. He said simply, "Getting older is tough, that's for sure. I'm sorry about your dad."

For a while both were quiet, and then Sam started talking again. "You know, back then I thought you were crazy. Now I don't know what to think. But it's like you got some secret or something. Kinda like you know something I don't know, or at least you think you do. It's not that I think you're playin' a game, or just acting like you got some special secret. No, I think you're sincere enough, but what I don't know is whether you're right or could be you're just duped. Not meaning to be rude, but there it is. And I might want to know the secret if a true secret there be, but I ain't joinin' a cult, know what I mean?"

Bob nodded understandingly. "You know, I had a hard time believing in The Manager and The Company at first, too. The truth is that even after I'd been in The Company for a while I was still sometimes struggling to figure it all out and to know what to believe. Then after a while the work itself became challenging, even overwhelming, and it seemed like things usually didn't go as smoothly as I thought they should. And the worst of it was that I was getting tired of working hard, especially not knowing for sure if anyone, especially The Manager, really cared or even noticed me much. And I felt like even if I worked hard, I might not really ever get anything worthwhile back. At that time I actually did have thoughts of returning to the diner, because I felt like giving up. The pay and benefits at the diner were lousy, but at least the expectations weren't so high. As long as I showed up most of the time and washed the dishes adequately enough, I got paid. Not a great life, but sometimes it did seem easier."

Bob wasn't really sure if it was a good idea to be telling Sam that life in The Company was difficult and even overwhelming at times to the point that he had considered giving up. *But what shall I say? Life in The Company is always a walk in the park? I can't deny the truth.*

"Really? You actually thought about coming back?"

"Yes, I really did." Bob paused reflectively, and considered carefully what he should say next. Then he said soberly, "Sam, I'm going to tell you the truth. The secret you are wondering about is simple. The Company is real. The Manager is real. And, he is completely trustworthy. It turned out my biggest problem in The Company was forgetting The Manager was my friend. When he helped me understand that, instead of returning to the diner, I turned back to him, and recommitted myself to him and to The Company. I've learned that even when work is difficult, he will always be there for me. That's been quite a few years ago now, and I have never really looked back since."

"Humph! Always there for you? Like even right now, far away from The Company, in an airplane flying miles above the earth? What if I decide to punch you in the snoot, he here to help you then?"

Both men laughed, and then Bob said, "The Company is different. It can't be contained by the walls of a building. It can't be contained by the programs and platitudes of men. Neither can The Manager."

On a hunch, Bob suddenly unfastened his seat belt and stood up. He looked around at all the passengers. A few seats back was the family he had been hearing. The young children were restless and complaining, occasionally even crying. The parents were trying to maintain control by appeasing them with snacks and toys. Most of the passengers looked like business travelers, both men and women. Some were likely heading off for a vacation or to visit family. All were occupied with reading or talking or even sleeping, and no one gave him more than a glance. At last Bob's eyes fell on the one passenger he was looking for. Seated near the back of the plane, The Manager smiled and nodded at Bob, and then he held something up, a small booklet.

Bob gave Sam a huge smile and said, "I think The Manager wants to see me for a minute."

Startled, Sam stared at Bob for a moment before unfastening his own seat belt and standing up. After a brief glance at the man holding up the booklet and smiling at them, he sat back down quickly. "Whoa! You gonna tell him I might punch you in the snoot?"

"Nah! I think he has something he wants me to give to you. I'll be back shortly." Bob made his way to the rear of the plane.

When he got there, The Manager said with a smile, "Good morning! Have a seat." After Bob was settled into the seat next to him, he said, "Don't worry about that report. You can work on it later in the hotel room when you don't have so much to do. Texting Amy was the right thing. Bob, I know you've been working very hard of late; it's been quite the uphill climb. You have persevered, and I am proud of you! Be sure to take advantage of little opportunities that come your way to relax and rest a bit. Now about Sam. What a coincidence, eh?"

Bob laughed a little and replied, "Not really a coincidence, I'm thinking."

"Would it surprise you to know that Sam has a sister who has been in my employ for a couple of years now? She has spoken to him on several occasions regarding The Company. There have been others as well who have labored before you. They went as far as they could, and in a very real sense, you are picking up where they left off. Sam's heart has been softened, and he is now ready to hear what you have to say. And Bob, don't feel like you have to say too much. Remember the goal is to get him talking to me personally."

The Manager handed Bob the booklet, something Bob was quite familiar with. He had been given a copy of it for himself on his first day with The Company, and The Manager had given him several copies since that day, each time asking him to be on the alert for someone else to give it to. It contained the basic tenets of life within The Company.

After Bob returned to his seat and got settled in, he looked at Sam with a raised eyebrow. "So, when were you going to tell me about your sister?"

Sam grimaced and said, "What's to say? She joined The Company a couple years ago. Been a real pain ever since, just like you."

The flight attendant was serving beverages and snacks, so the men lowered their trays. Bob placed the booklet The Manager had given him on the tray as he asked the attendant for a diet soda.

"You on a diet? Since when did you start drinking diet stuff?" To the attendant, Sam said, "I'll have a regular cola please." His tone suggested his was the only correct choice.

"I don't really need sugar in everything I drink. Besides, Amy's really a good cook. Helping myself to seconds every night is starting to show, you know?" Bob patted his stomach ruefully.

"Yeah, I can see that. You could complain to her about it. Maybe she'd put you on a diet of bread and water! That'd skinny you right up!" Both of them laughed and then Sam asked, "So, she pretty too? Or was it the cooking made you cave in and get hitched?"

"She's beautiful. So are my kids."

"Beautiful? You got pictures to back that up?"

Bob pulled out his phone and showed Sam a few pictures of Amy and the kids.

"Yeah, okay, I can see, they're beautiful! So, what's the reason for you to be on a plane without your beautiful family today? What kinda business do you do for The Company?"

How do I explain what I do in a way he can understand? "I work toward the promotion of The Company. I guess you could say it's publicizing."

"You make a lot of dough for The Company?"

"Mmmm, not really so much. What I do is valuable, but it's not really about the money."

"There's a lot about The Company that don't make sense. Ain't no company I know of values anything over money."

Bob nodded. "That's very true."

For a while they both ignored the booklet on Bob's tray, but at last Sam made a slight gesture toward it and said, "You know, my sis has tried to give me that a few times."

"Maybe you could accept it now just out of curiosity," Bob suggested somewhat teasingly. More seriously he added, "You know, she only tries to give it to you because she cares."

"Yeah, I know." Sam sighed. "I suppose you do too, or you wouldn't be bothering to try to get me to listen to you. The thing is, what I really can't figure out is what The Manager would need with one more employee, 'specially a guy like me."

"He has unlimited resources. He would have no problem carrying one more employee. Besides, it isn't that he needs you, Sam, it's that you need him."

"That's what Sis says, but I don't get it. Anyways, I'm so unqualified. I just don't get how he would ever get past that and hire me!"

"Sam, look at who you're talking to! It's me, Bob, the guy who washed dishes at the diner!"

"Yeah, that's another thing. I don't get how he hired you neither!"

"Hmm. I suppose you think The Company is filled with people who were hired on the basis of their qualifications, certifications, diplomas and all that fancy stuff."

"Course I do. What else would I think? That it's full of people who got hired because of their lack of any credentials?"

"Sam, I promise you, his grace is what it's all about, not our qualifications." After a short pause, he went on, "Sam, you know the story – about The Manager's death at the hands of that angry mob."

"Yeah, I know the story."

"Thing is, it's true. It's part of the secret. He didn't have to let that mob kill him, he chose dying on our behalf so that he could offer life to us in The Company, regardless of our qualifications. Sam, he did that for you!"

Sam stared dubiously at Bob for a few moments before he replied, "Sis has been saying that all along. I couldn't believe it, not from her. You see, she had all the fancy credentials. Unlike me, she worked hard in school and got herself an education. So I figured she earned the job they gave her. You're saying pretty much what she's been telling me, that no one gets hired on their own merit, not even someone like her. That what The Manager did, he did for all of us, even someone like me."

"Yep, that's what I'm saying."

"So it's possible that even a guy like me could get hired."

119

"Are you breathing?"

"Hmmm. The boss at the diner hires anyone who's breathing just because he needs workers. You're saying the opposite. You're saying The Manager hires anyone who's breathing because they need him."

"Yep, that's it."

Sam turned away and stared out the window again for a while. Then he turned back and asked, "So, is it worth it? I mean your whole life has changed. Sis says it's not about rules and regulations, but the end result is still that you don't do the same stuff you used to. Seems like I'd have to stop hanging out at bars and blowing off work every chance I get. And, you even said that work is sometimes really hard in The Company. So, what makes it worth giving up everything you're used to?"

"What makes it worth it? That's a really good question, Sam. It might be difficult to explain. But let me ask you this. Have you ever had a manager at any place you ever worked that actually cared about you? I mean sincerely and forever?"

"No, course not! I've had a few wanted to punch my lights out fer my laziness, that's about as personal as any ever got."

Bob chuckled. Then he asked, "And have you ever really considered your retirement benefits?"

"Retirement benefits? From the diner? Hah! That's a joke. I might get a few dollars back fer all my years of wearisome working and paying taxes. Likely it won't ever be enough to cover my needs. I think I'll be doing some sorta work 'til the day I die just to survive. And that'll be it. It's all kinda pointless and empty, you know?"

"I felt the same way. I never saved up much, and when I did manage to save a buck or two, some need for the money always happened along and it disappeared. On the other hand, The Manager has assured me that I will not be disappointed with my retirement package. He says he's preparing a place just for me, and that it's reserved for me already and nothing can ever touch it! I can't lose it and it can't fade away. Not only that, but it's more special than I can describe from what we in The Company have been told of it. I have to admit that knowing it's there is sometimes what gets me through the tough days at work. That's another one of those things that doesn't make sense from the usual perspective.

What other manager on the planet says he'll always be with you even in retirement? What other manager says he's preparing a special place for you that will last forever and you will be happy and never disappointed?"

"Shhh! Can't you see I'm trying to read?" Sam had picked up the booklet and opened it to the first page.

Bob smiled and leaned his seat back. Relaxing and closing his eyes, he thought things over. He'd sent his text to Amy. The report could wait until later. Sam was reading. It had been a long week already, and it wasn't over yet. *I'm tired. The Manager said to watch for restful opportunities. I just need a few minutes to close my eyes.*

The next thing Bob knew, he had somehow left the plane and was floating through a blue sky dotted with white clouds. Then just as suddenly he was walking through a meadow lush with grass. Wildflowers were everywhere. Birds were chirping and butterflies floated about and danced on the flowers. Suddenly he saw Amy and the kids walking through the flowers toward him. They were smiling and looked so happy. He hugged Amy tightly, and they both laughed as they watched the kids chase the butterflies. *But where's The Manager?* He saw him then, coming toward them, smiling and somehow looking more radiant than the sunshine.

www.ingramcontent.com/pod-product-compliance
Lightning Source LLC
Chambersburg PA
CBHW060637130626
46555CB00002B/836